A LITTLE COUNTRY GIRL

BY

SUSAN COOLIDGE

British Library Cataloguing-in-Publication Data
A catalogue record for this book is available from the
British Library

Contents

Sarah Chauncey Woolsey

Sarah Chauncey Woolsey was born on 29 January 1835, into a wealthy and influential New England Dwight family, in Cleveland, Ohio, USA. Woolsey spent much of her early years in New Haven, Connecticut, after her family moved there in 1852. But soon, she craved a more independent life, away from her relatives, and worked as a nurse during the American Civil War (1861-1865). Her time as a medical worker provided Woolsey with the experience and self-determination in order to embark on her writing career. She has subsequently become famous as a children's author, writing numerous books under the pseudonym of 'Susan Coolidge'. Woolsey is best known for her classic children's novel What Katy Did (published in 1872), which follows the adventures of a small American girl, Katy Carr, who lives in the fictional lakeside Ohio town of Burnet. The protagonist is based on Woolsey herself, with the rest of the family, most notably the brothers and sisters, modelled on her four younger siblings. The substantial success of this book meant that Woolsey was able to produce a popular series of 'Katy' books, the last of which was published in 1890. Woolsey also wrote numerous short stories, poems, and a plethora of children's novels (48 poems and 37 books in total). Woolsey never married, and resided at her family home in Newport,

Rhode Island, until her death. She died on 9 April, 1905, at the age of seventy.

The Staircase Window.
Candace settled herself for a long, comfortable reading before breakfast.

CHAPTER I.
ON THE "EOLUS."

It was on one of the cool, brilliant days which early June brings to the Narragansett country, that the steamer "Eolus" pushed out from Wickford Pier on her afternoon trip to Newport. The sky was of a beautiful translucent blue; the sunshine had a silvery rather than a golden radiance. A sea-wind blew up the Western Passage, so cool as to make the passengers on the upper deck glad to draw their wraps about them. The low line of the mainland beyond Conanicut and down to Beaver Tail glittered with a sort of clear-cut radiance, and seemed lifted a little above the water. Candace Arden heard the Captain say that he judged, from the look of things, that there was going to be a change of weather before long.

Captain Peleg King was a great favorite on his line of travel. He had a pleasant, shrewd face, grizzled hair, a spare, active figure; and he seemed to notice every one of his passengers and to take an interest in them.

"Going down to Newport, Miss?" he said to Candace, after giving her one or two quick looks.

The question was superfluous, for the "Eolus" went nowhere else except to Newport; but it was well-meant, for the Captain thought that Candace seemed lonely and ill at ease, and he wished to cheer her.

"Yes, sir," she answered, shyly.

"Your folks there for the summer?" he went on.

"No, sir; I'm going to stay with my cousin Mrs. Gray."

"Mrs. Courtenay Gray you mean, I guess. Well, it's queer, but I sort er thought that you favored her a little. She's down early this year. I fetched her and the family across on my evening trip more 'n two weeks ago. Mrs. Gray's a mighty nice lady; I'm always pleased when she comes aboard. Wouldn't you like to take a seat in the wheel-house, Miss? The wind's blowing pretty fresh."

Candace was not aware that this was a distinguishing attention which the Captain did not pay everybody, and which she owed partly to her connection with Mrs. Gray and partly to her solitary look, which had touched Captain Peleg's benevolent heart. He had a girl of his own "over to Wickford," who was about the same age; and it made him "kind of tender" toward other girls who didn't seem to have any one to look after them. But the wind was fresh, and it was pleasant to be spoken to and noticed by some one on this, the first long journey of her short life; so she thankfully accepted the Captain's invitation, and let him escort her along the deck, and assist her to mount the two steps which led into the wheel-house.

It was rather a pleasant-looking place in which she found herself. Three sides of the little enclosure were lined with windows, through which the green shores, which seemed to be rapidly drifting past them, could be seen. The fourth side was filled with a long cushioned bench. In the middle of the glassed front was the big brass wheel, shining with polish and friction, and revolving artistically in the hands of its steersman, who kept his eye fixed alternately on the water and on his compass. There seemed to be no regulation against speaking to this "man at the wheel," or if there were, it was not strictly regarded; for two young ladies, who were already ensconced in one corner of the long seat, were plying him with all manner of questions.

They were rather pretty girls of that hard modern type which carries the air of knowing everything worth the knowing, having a right to everything worth the having, and being fully determined to claim that right to its fullest extent. As Candace entered, they favored her with one rapid, scrutinizing glance that took in every detail of her apparel, from the goat-skin boots which were too large for her feet to the round hat whose every bow bore witness to a country milliner, and after that they noticed her no more.

She, for her part, only too glad to be left unnoticed, looked shyly out of the corners of her eyes at them. They seemed to her inexpressibly stylish; for their tailor-made suits, though almost as plain as her own dress and jacket of blue alpaca, had that perfect fit and finish which makes the simplest dress seem all that can be desired. There was a knowing look to each little detail, from the slender silver bangles which appeared beneath the loose wrinkled wrists of their very long gloves to the tortoise-shell pins with which their hats were fastened to the tightly braided hair coiled low down on the nape of the neck. Candace's hair fell in curls to her waist. She had always worn it so, and no one had ever thought anything about it; but now, all in a moment, she felt that it was wrong and improper.

"Been up to New York, Miss Joy?" said the Captain.

"No; only as far as the Junction, to meet a friend," replied the prettier of the two girls. "Why weren't you on the boat this morning, Captain?"

"I was on the boat. I never miss a trip, except sometimes the night one in the summer-time, when the sleeping-train is a running. I don't always come over in that. Let me see, how did I come to miss you to-day?"

"Oh, I sat in the ladies' cabin all the way, not on deck. But I didn't see you when we landed."

"Well, I don't know how it happened, I'm sure. Are your folks down for the season?"

"Yes: that is, mamma and I and my brother are here; my married sister won't come till next month." Then she turned to her friend, but without lowering her voice.

"You can't think how dull it's been, Ethel: no men, no dinners; nothing going on as yet. The Casino is only just opened, and people haven't begun to go there. We tried to get up a tennis match, but there weren't enough good players to make it worth while. There's absolutely nothing. Mrs. Courtenay Gray had a girls' lunch on Tuesday; but that is all, and that didn't count for much."

"That's Georgie Gray's mother, isn't it? Is she there?"

"Oh, yes,—she and Gertrude, all the Grays. They're as nice and delightful as can be, of course, but somehow they're so literary and quiet, and Mrs. Gray is awfully particular about the girls. She makes them keep on with studying all summer, and she's so exclusive,—she won't let them visit half the new people."

"Gracious! why not?"

"Oh, I don't know,—she says they're not good form, and all that; but I'm sure she knows queer people enough herself. There is that tiresome old Miss Gisborne down in Washington Street,—the girls are forever going there; and I've seen them myself ever so many times coming out of the Hares',—and they take boarders!"

"Fancy! How extraordinary! Oh, there are the frigates!"

For the "Eolus," leaving the wooded, wall-like bank of Gould's Island behind, and rounding a point, had now reached the small curving bay to the eastward of Coasters'

Harbor, where lay the training-ships, the "New Hampshire" and the "Minnesota." It was a beautiful sight,—the two great war-vessels at anchor, with their tall tapering spars and flying flags reflected in the water on which they floated. Lines of glinting white flashed along the decks; for it was "wash-day," and the men's clothes were drying in the sun. Two or three barges were disembarking visitors at the gangway ladders, and beyond them a sail-boat was waiting its turn to do the same. On the pier a file of blue-uniformed boys were marching with measured tread. The sound of their feet came across the distance like the regular beat of a machine. A girl in a row-boat was just pushing out from the farther beach, above which rose a stone house covered with vines.

"That's Miss Isherwood," said one of the young ladies. "She's a splendid rower, and Tom says she swims as well as he does."

The whole scene was like enchantment to Candace, who had lived all her life among the hills of Connecticut, and had never till that day seen the ocean. She was much too shy to ask questions, but she sat like one in a dream, taking in with wide-open eyes all the details of the charming view,—the shores, broken by red-roofed villas and cottages rising from clouds of leafy greenery; the Torpedo Island with its tall flag-staff and floating banner over the dwelling of the Commandant; Fort Adams, whose steep glacis seemed powdered with snow just then from the multitude of daisies in bloom upon them; the light-houses; the soft rises of hill; and beyond, the shimmering heave of the open sea. Cat-boats and yachts flitted past in the fair wind like large white-winged moths; row-boats filled with pleasure-parties dipped their oars in the wake of the "Eolus;" steam-launches with screeching whistles were putting into their docks, among old boat-houses and warehouses, painted dull-red, or turned of a blackish gray by years of exposure to weather. Behind rose Newport, with the graceful spire of Trinity Church and the long bulk of the Ocean House surmounting the quaint buildings on the lower hill. The boat was heading toward a wharf, black with carriages, which were evidently drawn up to wait the arrival of the "Eolus."

"There's Mrs. Gray's team now, Miss," said the sharp-eyed Captain; "come down for you, I reckon."

The two girls glanced at her and then at each other. They shrugged their shoulders, and Candace heard one of them whisper,—

"Did you ever?" and the reply, "No; but after all, we didn't say anything very bad, and who would have dreamed that a hat like that had anything to do with the Grays?"

She felt herself blush painfully. The hat was a new one of brown straw trimmed with dark blue ribbon. She had felt rather proud of it when it came home from the milliner's the day before, and had considered the little blue pompon with which Miss Wilson, who was authority in matters of fashion in North Tolland, had enriched the middle bow, as a masterpiece of decoration. Alas! the apple of knowledge was at her lips; already she felt herself blush at the comments of these unknown girls whose hats were so different from her own, and was thoroughly uncomfortable, though she could hardly have told why.

Captain Peleg politely carried her bag for her across the landing-plank to where the "team," a glossy coupé with one horse, was waiting. He beckoned to the smart coachman, who wore a dark green overcoat with big metal buttons, to draw nearer.

"Here's your passenger," he said, helping Candace into the carriage. "Good-day, Miss. I hope we'll see you again on the 'Eolus.' All right, driver."

"Oh, thank you," cried Candace, finding voice and forgetting shyness in her gratitude; "you've been real kind to me, Captain."

"That child's got mighty pretty eyes," soliloquized Captain King, as he marched down the wharf. "I wonder what relation she is to the Grays. She don't seem their sort exactly. She's been raised in the country, I expect; but Mrs. Gray'll polish her up if anybody can, or I'm mistaken. Steady there—what're you about?" as a trunk came bounding and ricochetting across the gangway; "this wharf ain't no skittle-ground!"

Meanwhile the coupé was slowly climbing a steep side-street which led to the Avenue. Looking forth with observant eyes, Candace noted how the houses, which at first were of the last-century build, with hipped roofs and dormer windows like those to which she was accustomed in the old hill village that had been her birthplace, gave way to modernized old houses with recent additions, and then to houses which were unmistakably new, and exhibited all manner of queer peaks and pinnacles and projections, shingled, painted in divers colors, and broken by windows of oddly tinted glass. Next the carriage passed a modern church built of pinkish-brown stone; and immediately after, the equable roll of the wheels showed that they were on a smooth macadamized road. It was, in fact, though Candace did not know it, the famous Bellevue Avenue, which in summer is the favorite drive for all fashionable persons, and thronged from end to end on every fair afternoon by all manner of vehicles, from dainty pony-wagons to enormous mail-coaches.

There were only a few carriages in sight now, though they seemed many to our little country maid. Shops were opening for the season. Men were busy in hanging Eastern rugs and curtains up to view, and arranging in the windows beautiful jars and plates of porcelain and pottery, glittering wares from Turkey and Damascus, carved furniture, and inlaid cabinets. Half a dozen florists exhibited masses of hot-house flowers amid a tangle of palms and tree-ferns;

beyond was the announcement of an "opening" by a well-known dressmaker, whose windows were hung with more beautiful things than Candace in her small experience had ever dreamed of before,—laces, silks, embroideries.

The shops gave way to houses, each set in a court-yard gay with newly planted beds of flowers or foliage plants. Vines clustered everywhere; the trees, not yet fully in leaf, were like a tossing spray of delicate fresh green: a sense of hope, of expectation, of something delightful which was being prepared for, seemed to be in the air.

Suddenly the coupé turned in between a pair of substantial stone gate-posts, and drew up before a large square house, with piazzas on two sides, and a small but very smooth lawn, whose closely cut grass looked like green velvet. It was dappled with weeping-trees and evergreens, and hedged with a high wall of shrubs which shut off the view of the street. A continuous flower-bed ran all round the house close to its walls, planted full of geraniums, heliotrope, nasturtiums, mignonette, and pansies. Every window and balcony boasted its box of ferns or flowers; and in spite of the squareness of the building, and the sombre green-gray with which it was painted, the general effect was of cheerfulness, and shade broken by color,—an effect which is always pleasant.

Candace had forgotten herself in the excitement of new sights and experiences; but her shyness came back with a rush as the carriage stopped and the door was opened by a very smart French butler.

"Is Mrs. Gray at home?" she asked timidly, bending forward.

"Descendez, Mademoiselle, s'il vous plaît. Madame est occupée pour le moment; il y a du monde dans le salon." Then, seeing the perplexed look in Candace's eyes, he explained in broken English: "Mees is to get out. Madame is beesy with coompany for little while. Mees will please go up-stair."

Candace got out; the carriage drove away, and she followed the butler into the hall. He gave a low call at the foot of the stairs, which brought down a ladies'-maid with a ruffed cap perched on the back of her head.

"This way, if you please, Miss," she said, and led Candace up the staircase, which was a wide one with three square turns and a broad landing, lit with a range of windows and furnished with a low cushioned seat; then came an upper hall, and she was shown into a pretty corner room.

"If you'll please sit down and rest yourself, Miss," said the maid, "Mrs. Gray'll be up as soon as some company she has is gone. Would you like to have a cup of tea, Miss?"

"No, thank you," faltered Candace; and then the maid went away, shutting the door behind her.

The room, which had no bed in it, and was, in fact, Mrs. Gray's morning-room, was so full of curious things that

Candace's first thought was that it would take a week at least to see half that was in it. The sage-green walls were thickly hung with photographs, watercolors, charcoal sketches, miniatures, bits of faience, lacquered trays and discs, and great shining circles of Syrian and Benares metalwork. There were many pieces of pottery of various sorts, set here and there, on the chimney-piece, on book-shelves, on the top of a strangely carved black cabinet, with hinges and handles of wrought iron. In one corner stood an Italian spinning-wheel of ebony and silver; in another an odd instrument, whose use Candace could not guess, but which was in reality a Tyrolean zither. An escritoire, drawn near a window, was heaped with papers and with writing appliances of all sorts, and all elegant. There were many little tables covered with books and baskets of crewels and silks, and easy-chairs of every description. Every chair-back and little stand had some quaint piece of lace-work or linen-work thrown over it. It was, in fact, one of those rooms belonging distinctly to our modern life, for the adornment of which every part of the world is ransacked, and their products set forth in queer juxtapositions, to satisfy or to exhibit the varied tastes and pursuits of its occupants. To Candace it was as wonderful as any museum; and while her eyes slowly travelled from one object to another, she forgot her strangeness and was happy.

Tick, tick, tick, tick, went the little French clock on the mantelpiece. Suddenly it struck her that it was a long while that she had been left alone in this room. She glanced at the clock; it really was almost an hour. All her latent homesickness returned with fresh force. Her eyes filled with sudden tears; in another moment she would have been actually crying, but just then came a quick step, a little rustle, and she had just time to wipe away the drops when the door opened, and Mrs. Gray hurried into the room.

"My poor child," she exclaimed, "have you been alone all this time? It is quite too bad! I made sure that I should hear the carriage drive up, and at least run out and give you a welcome, but somehow I didn't; and people came so fast and thick that I couldn't get a chance to glance at the clock." She kissed Candace, and looked at her with a sort of soft scrutiny. It was to the full as penetrating as that of the strange girls on the steamer had been; but it did not hurt like theirs. Mrs. Gray had beautiful, big, short-sighted blue eyes with black lashes; when she smiled they seemed to brim with a sudden fascinating radiance. She smiled now, and reminded Candace somehow of a great, soft, fully opened garden rose.

"You have something of your mother's looks, Cannie," she said. "I knew her best when she was about your age. I never saw much of her after she married your father and went up to live among the hills." She sighed softly: there was a short pause. Then, with a sudden change of tone, she continued: "And all this time you have never been shown your room. I can't think why they were so stupid. Who was it put you here, Cannie?"

"It was—a lady—in a cap," replied Candace, hesitatingly.

"A lady?—cap? Oh, it must have been Elizabeth. She's my maid,—don't make such a mistake again, dear; you must learn to discriminate. Well, come with me now, and let me see you comfortably established. The girls are gone on a yachting-party to the upper end of the island. It was an old engagement, made before your aunt's letter came, or they would not have been absent when you arrived. They were very sor—"

But in the very middle of the word came Frederic, the butler, with the announcement of new visitors; and, just taking time to lead Candace down the entry to a room whose door stood wide open, Mrs. Gray hurried away, saying rapidly: "Take off your hat, dear. Lie down for a rest, hadn't you better? I'll be up again presently."

"I wonder if everybody is always in a hurry in Newport?" Candace thought.

She was again alone, but this time she felt no disposition to cry. Her trunk had been brought up by somebody, and stood already in its place, with the straps unloosened. She took off her hat and jacket, unpacked a little, and peeped out of the window to see where she was. The room faced the east, and across a corner of the lawn and the stable-yard she had a glimpse of the sea, which had become intensely blue with the coming of the later afternoon.

"Oh, that is good," she said to herself. "I shall see it all summer." She glanced about the room with a growing sense of proprietorship which was pleasant. It was not a large room, but it looked cheerful, with its simple furniture of pale-colored ash and a matted floor, over which lay a couple of Persian rugs. There was a small fireplace bordered with blue tiles which matched the blue papering on the walls; and the tiles on the washstand, and the chintz of the easy-chair and lounge, and the flower-jars on the mantelpiece were blue also. Altogether it was a pretty little chamber, with which any girl might be sufficiently well-pleased; and as Candace noticed the tiny nosegay of mignonette and tea-roses which stood on the bureau, her heart lightened with the sense that it had been put there for her. Some one had thought of her coming, and prepared for it.

She brushed out her curls and washed her face and hands, but did not change her dress. The blue alpaca was the newest she had, and she wished to look her best on that first evening. She sat down in the window to listen to the soft boom of the surf, which seemed to grow louder as the night drew on, and did not hear Mrs. Gray as she came down the entry. That lady stood a moment in the half-open door, surveying her young visitor.

"What am I to do with her?" she thought. "I want to befriend Candace's child, but I did not quite realize, till I saw her just now, what a disadvantage she would be at among all these girls here, with their French clothes and their worse than French ideas. She's not plain. There's a good deal of beauty about that shy little face of hers, and refinement too, if only she were not so awkward. If I can once get her into a dress that fits, and do something with that mop of curls, she would look well enough. I wonder if she will take it kindly, or flare up and feel offended at every little suggestion. That would be terrible!— You are listening to the surf, dear. I'm afraid it means rain to-morrow. That sound generally is a symptom of mischief."

"Is it?" said Candace; "what a pity!"

"A pity about the rain?"

"No—but it's such a pretty sound."

"So it is. Well, if you are ready, let us go downstairs. I expect the girls every moment. Ah, there they are now!"

The line of windows on the staircase landing commanded a view of the gate and approach, and looking through them Candace saw a village cart with two girls on the front seat, one driving, and a third girl in the rumble behind, approaching the house. A couple of young men on horseback rode close beside the cart. One of them jumped from his horse, helped the young ladies out, there was a moment of laughter and chat; then, touching their hats, the riders departed, and the three girls came into the hall.

"Mamma! mammy! where are you, dear?" sang out three youthful voices.

"Here I am, half-way upstairs," replied Mrs. Gray, seating herself on the cushioned bench of the landing.

"What on earth are you doing up there? And who's that with you?"

"It's your cousin Candace. Come up and be introduced."

Up they came at a run, each trying to be the first to arrive. Candace had never known many girls, but these were of a different species from any she had seen before. They seemed full of spirits, and conveyed the idea of being, so to speak, bursting with happiness, though I suppose not one of the three but would have resented the imputation of being happier than people in general are or ought to be. Georgie, the eldest, was short and round, and had her mother's blue near-sighted eyes without her mother's beauty. Gertrude was unusually tall, and had a sort of lily-like grace; her light hair was very thick, and so fine in quality that it stood out like a nimbus round her pale pretty face. Little Marian, the youngest, two years Candace's junior, was not yet in society, but had been allowed to go to the picnic as a great favor. Her hair had a reddish tint in its chestnut, and was braided in one large plait down her back; she had brown eyes and a capable little face which was full of expression.

They all spoke kindly to Candace, they all kissed her, but she felt much less at ease with them than with their mother, whose peculiarly charming manner seemed to invite confidence from everybody. After a few questions and a few words of welcome, they plunged into a description of their picnic,—the yacht-sail, the landing, the luncheon, the general delightfulness of everything.

"Berry Joy was not there," remarked Georgie. "She had gone up to Wickford to meet some one. By the way, she must have come down on the 'Eolus' with you, Candace. Did you see her?"

"There were two young ladies," answered Candace, timidly.

"Did you hear their names? Did you talk to them?" asked Gertrude.

"No—yes—no—I mean the Captain called one of them Miss Joy. I didn't talk to them, but they knew you."

"Why, how could you tell that?"

"I heard them talking about you."

"What fun! What did they say?"

Candace hesitated. Her face grew crimson. "I'd rather—I don't—" she began. Then with a great effort, rallying her powers, she went on: "I didn't like to sit there and hear them and not tell them that I was your cousin; but

I was too—too—frightened to speak to them, so I thought I would never repeat what they said, and then it wouldn't be any matter."

"Quite right, Cannie," said Mrs. Gray, quickly. Something in the girl's little speech seemed to please her very much.

CHAPTER II.
THE FIRST EVENING.

CANDACE ARDEN'S mother had not only been Mrs. Gray's cousin, but her particular friend as well. The two girls had been brought up together, had shared their studies and secrets and girlish fun, and had scarcely ever been separated for a week, until suddenly a change came which separated them for all the rest of their lives.

Pretty Candace Van Vliet went up to New Haven on her nineteenth birthday to see what a college commencement was like, and at the President's reception afterward met Henry Arden, the valedictorian of the graduating class, a handsome fellow just twenty-one years old. He came of plain farming-people in the hill country of Connecticut; but he was clever, ambitious, and his manners had a natural charm, to which his four years of college life had added ease and the rubbing away of any little rustic awkwardness with which he might have begun. Candace thought him delightful; he thought her more than delightful. In short, it was one of the sudden love-affairs with which college commencements not infrequently end, and in the course of a few weeks they engaged themselves to each other.

Henry was to be a minister, and his theological course must be got through with before they could marry. Three years the course should have taken, but he managed to do it in a little more than two, being spurred on by his impatient desire for home and wife, and a longing, no less urgent, to begin as soon as possible to earn his own bread and relieve his father from the burden of his support. No one knew better than he with what pinching and saving and self-sacrifice it had been made possible for him to get a college education and become a clergyman; what daily self-denials had been endured for his sake in that old yellow farm-house on the North Tolland hills. He was the only son, the only child; and his father and mother were content to bear anything so long as it gave him a chance to make the most of himself.

It is not an uncommon story in this New England of ours. Many and many a farm-house could tell a similar tale of thrift, hard work, and parental love. The bare rocky acres are made to yield their uttermost, the cows to do their full duty, the scanty apples of the "off year" are carefully harvested, every pullet and hen is laid under contribution for the great need of the moment,—the getting the boys through college. It is both beautiful and pitiful, as all sacrifices must be; but the years of effort and struggle do not always end, as in the case of the Ardens, with a disappointment and a grief so bitter as to make the self-spending seem all in vain.

For the over-study of those two years proved too much for Henry Arden's health. It was not hard study alone; he stinted himself in food, in firing as well; he exacted every possible exertion from his mind, and systematically neglected his body. The examinations were brilliantly passed; he was ordained; he received a "call" to Little Upshire, the village nearest to North Tolland; there was a pretty wedding in the old Van Vliet mansion on Second Avenue, at which Kate Van Vliet, herself just engaged to Courtenay Gray, acted as bridesmaid; and then the cousins parted. They only met once again, when Mrs. Arden came down from the country to see her cousin married. Henry did not come with her; he was not very well, she explained, and she must hurry back.

That was the beginning of a long wasting illness. Some spring of vitality seemed to have been broken during those two terrible years at the theological seminary; and though Henry Arden lived on, and even held his parish for several years, he was never fit for any severe study or labor. The last three years of his life were spent in the old farm-house at North Tolland, where his aunt Myra, a spare, sinewy, capable old maid, was keeping house for his father. Mrs. Arden had died soon after her son's illness began; her heart was "kind of broken," the neighbors said, and perhaps it was.

And little Candace and her mother lived on with the old people after the long, sorrowful nursing was done, and another gray headstone had been placed beside the rest in the Arden lot in the North Tolland graveyard, having carved upon it, "Sacred to the memory of the Rev. Henry Arden, aged thirty-four. The Lord gave, and the Lord hath taken away. Blessed be His Holy name." There seemed nothing else for them to do but to live on where they were. Mrs. Gray was in China with her husband, who at that time was the resident partner in a well-known firm of tea-importers. Aunt Van Vliet had gone to Europe after her daughter's marriage. There was no one to come to the aid of the drooping young widow, and carry her away from the lonely life and the sad memories which were slowly killing her. For her child's sake she did her best to rally; but her strength had been severely taxed during her husband's illness, and dying was easier than living; so she died when Candace was just eight years old, and the little girl and the two old people were left alone in the yellow farm-house.

A twelvemonth later, Grandfather Arden had a stroke of paralysis.—Don't be too much discouraged, dear children; this is positively the last death that I shall have occasion to chronicle in this story. But it seemed necessary to show what sort of life Candace had lived, in order to explain the sort of girl she was.—After her grandfather died, Aunt Myra, aged sixty-nine, and little Cannie, aged nine, alone remained of the once large household; and the farm-house seemed very big and empty, and had strange echoes in all the unused corners.

It was a lonely place, and a lonely life for a child. Candace had few enjoyments, and almost no young companions. She had never been used to either, so she did not feel the want of them as most little girls would have done. Aunt Myra was kind enough, and, indeed, fond of her in a dry, elderly way; but she could not turn herself into a play-mate. It is not often that a person who is as old as sixty-nine remembers how it feels to play. Aunt Myra approved of Cannie especially, because she was "such a quiet child;" but I think Cannie's mother would rather have had her noisier.

"She's a nice girl as I want to see," Aunt Myra was wont to tell her cronies. "She's likely-appearing enough,—and that's better than being too pretty. And she's helpful about the house for such a young cretur, and she's not a bit forth-putting or highty-tighty. I don't know how I should have managed if Candace had turned out the sort of girl some of 'em are,—like those Buell girls, for instance, always raising Ned because they can't get down to Hartford or Bridgeport to shop and see the sights and have a good time. As if good times couldn't be had to home as well as anywhere! Why, I reckon that Miss Buell has more fuss and trouble in fitting out those girls every spring of her life than I've had with Cannie since her mother died. She never makes one mite of difficulty, or bothers with objections. She just puts on whatever I see fit to get her; and she likes it, and there's the end."

This was not quite as true as Aunt Myra supposed. Candace wore whatever it was ordained that she should wear, but she did not always "like" it. From her mother she inherited a certain instinct of refinement and taste which only needed the chance to show itself. But there was little chance to exercise taste in the old yellow farm-house, and Candace, from training and long habit, was submissive; so she accepted the inevitable, and, as her great-aunt said, "made no difficulty."

Letters came now and then from "Cousin Kate," far away in China, and once a little box with a carved ivory fan as fine as lace-work, a dozen gay pictures on rice paper, and a scarf of watermelon-pink crape, which smelt of sandalwood, and was by far the most beautiful thing that Cannie had ever seen. Then, two years before our story opens, the Grays came back to America to live; and a correspondence began between Mrs. Gray and Aunt Myra, part of which Candace heard about and part she did not. Mrs. Gray was anxious to know her cousin's child and be of use to her; but first one thing and then another delayed their meeting. The first winter the Grays spent at a hotel looking for a house; the second, they were all in Florida on account of Mr. Gray's health. These difficulties were now settled. A town house had been chosen, a Newport cottage leased for a term of years, and Cannie was asked for a long summer visit.

It was Mrs. Gray's secret desire that this visit should lead to a sort of adoption, that Cannie should stay on with them as a fourth daughter, and share all her cousins' advantages of education and society; but before committing herself to such a step, she wished to see what the girl was like.

"It's so much easier to keep out of such an arrangement than to get out of it," she told her husband. "My poor Candace was an angel, all sweetness and charm; but her child has the blood of those stiff Connecticut farmers in her. She may be like her father's people, and not in the least like her mother; she may be hopelessly stupid or vulgar or obstinate or un-improvable. We will wait and see."

This secret doubt and question was, I think, the reason why Mrs. Gray was so pleased at Cannie's little speech about Miss Joy and her friend.

"That was the true, honorable feeling," she thought to herself; "the child is a lady by instinct. It wasn't easy for her to say it, either; she's a shy little thing. Well, if she has the instinct, the rest can be added. It's easy enough to polish a piece of mahogany, but you may rub all day at a pine stick and not make much out of it."

As these thoughts passed rapidly through her mind, she stole her arm across Candace's shoulders and gave them a little warm pressure; but all she said was,—

"Dinner in twenty minutes, children. You would better run up at once and make ready. Cannie, you and I will go to the library,—you haven't seen my husband yet."

The library was a big, airy room, with an outlook to the sea. There were not many books in it, only enough to fill a single low range of book-shelves; but the tables were covered with freshly cut magazines and pamphlet novels; there was a great file of "Punch" and other illustrated papers, and that air of light-reading-in-abundance which seems to suit a house in summer-time. A little wood-fire was snapping on a pair of very bright andirons, and, June though it was, its warmth was agreeable. Beside it, in an enormous Russia-leather armchair, sat Mr. Gray,—an iron-whiskered, shrewd-looking man of the world, with a pair of pleasant, kindly eyes, and that shining bald spot on his head which seems characteristic of the modern business man.

"Court, here is our new child," said Mrs. Gray; "poor Candace's daughter, you know."

Mr. Gray understood, from his wife's tone, that she was pleased with her little visitor so far, and he greeted her in a very friendly fashion.

"You have your mother's eyes," he said. "I recollect her perfectly, though we only met two or three times, and that was seventeen—let me see—nearly eighteen years ago it must have been. Her hair, too, I should say," glancing at Cannie's chestnut mop; "it was very thick, I remember, and curled naturally."

"Aunt Myra always says that my hair is the same color as mother's," replied Candace.

"It is almost exactly the same. Do you remember her at all, Cannie?" asked Mrs. Gray.

"Just a little. I recollect things she used to wear, and where she used to sit, and one or two things she said. But perhaps I don't recollect them, but think I do because Aunt Myra told them to me."

"Is there no picture of her?"

"Only a tin-type, and it isn't very good. It's almost faded out; you can hardly see the face."

"What a pity!"

"Le dîner est servi, Madame," said the voice of Frederic at the door.

"We won't wait for the girls. They will be down in a moment," said Mrs. Gray, as she led the way to the dining-room. The sound of their feet on the staircase was heard as she spoke; and down they ran, the elder two in pretty dresses of thin white woollen stuff, which Candace in her unworldliness thought fine enough for a party.

People in North Tolland did not dine in the modern sense of the word. They took in supplies of food at stated intervals, very much as a locomotive stops for wood and water when it cannot go on any longer without such replenishment; but it was a matter of business and necessity to do so rather than of pleasure.

Candace, who had sat down opposite Aunt Myra every day as long as she could remember at the small pine table in the yellow-painted kitchen, with always the same thick iron-stone ware plates and cups, the same little black tray to hold the tea-things, the same good, substantial, prosaic fare, served without the least attempt at grace or decoration, had never dreamed of such a dinner as was usual at the Grays'. She said not a word to express her astonishment; but she glanced at the thick cluster of maiden-hair ferns which quivered in the middle of the table from an oval stand of repoussé brass, at the slender glasses of tea-roses which stood on either side, at the Sèvres dishes of fruit, sweet biscuits, and dried ginger, and wondered if this were to be all the dinner. Did fashionable people never eat anything more substantial than grapes and crackers? She felt very hungry, and yet it seemed coarse not to be satisfied when everything was so pretty.

"Consommé, Mademoiselle?" murmured Frederic in her ear, as he placed before her a plate full of some clear liquid which smelt deliciously, and offered a small dish of grated cheese for her acceptance.

"Oh, thank you, sir," said Candace, wondering confusedly if cheese in soup was the correct thing.

Mrs. Gray's quick ear caught the "sir." She did not even turn her head, but she mentally added another to the hints which must be administered to Candace as soon as she was sufficiently at home to bear them.

Spanish mackerel was the next course. Candace inadvertently took up the steel knife placed beside her plate, instead of the silver one meant for use with fish. The result was that when the saddle of mutton was served, she had no usable knife. Mr. Gray observed her difficulty, and directed Frederic to bring a steel knife for Mademoiselle, which Frederic did, first casting a scrutinizing glance about as if in search of something; and again Candace felt that she was somehow out of the way.

The climax of her discomfort came with the pretty tinted fruit plates and finger-bowls. Candace's tumbler was empty, and without particularly thinking about the matter she took a drink out of her finger-bowl, which she mistook for some sort of lemonade, from the bit of lemon which floated in the water.

The moment after, she was conscious of her blunder. She saw Georgie dabbling her fingers in her bowl. She saw Gertrude with difficulty keeping back a smile which would flicker in her eyes, though her lips were rigidly grave. Little Marian giggled outright, and then relapsed into a frightened solemnity. Candace felt utterly miserable. She looked toward Mrs. Gray apprehensively, but that lady only gave her an encouraging smile. Mr. Gray put a bunch of hot-house grapes on her plate. She ate them without the least idea of their flavor. With the last grape a hot tear splashed down; and the moment Mrs. Gray moved, Candace fled upstairs to her own room, where she broke down into a fit of homesick crying.

How she longed for the old customary home among the hills, where nobody minded what she did, or how she ate, or "had any manners in particular," as she phrased it to her own mind, or thought her ignorant or awkward. And yet, on sober second thought, did she really wish so much to go back? Was it not better to stay on where she was, and learn to be graceful and low-spoken and at ease always, like her cousin Kate, if she could, even if she had to undergo some mortification in the process? Candace was not sure.

She had stopped crying, and was cooling her eyes with a wet towel when she heard a little tap at the door. It was Mrs. Gray herself.

"Where are you, Cannie?" she said, looking about the room with her short-sighted eyes. "You are so dark here that I cannot see you."

"I'm here by the washstand," faltered Candace; and then, to her dismay, she began to cry again. She tried to subdue it; but a little sob, which all her efforts could not stifle, fell upon her cousin's observant ear.

"My dear child, you are crying," she exclaimed; and in another minute Candace, she scarcely knew how, was in Mrs. Gray's arms, they were sitting on the sofa together, and she was finishing her cry with her head on the kindest of shoulders and an unexpected feeling of comfort at her heart. Anything so soft and tender as Cousin Kate's arms she had never known before; there was a perfume of motherliness about them which to a motherless girl was wholly irresistible. Gertrude declared that mamma always stroked people's trouble away with those hands of hers, and that they looked just like the hands of the Virgin in Holbein's Madonna, as if they could mother the whole world.

"Now, tell me, Cannie, tell me, dear child," said Mrs. Gray, when the shower was over and the hard sobs had grown faint and far between, "what made you cry? Was it because you are tired and a little homesick among us all, or were you troubled about anything? Tell me, Cannie."

"Oh, it's only because I'm so stupid and—and—countrified," said Candace, beginning to sob again. "I made such horrid mistakes at dinner, and Gertrude wanted to laugh,—she didn't laugh, but I saw her want to,—and Marian did laugh, and I felt so badly."

"Marian is such a little girl that you must forgive her this once," said Mrs. Gray, "though I am rather ashamed of her myself. I saw all your 'mistakes,' as you call them, Cannie, even one or two that you didn't see yourself. They were very little mistakes, dear, not worth crying about,—small blunders in social etiquette, which is a matter of minor importance,—not failures in good feeling or good manners, which are of real consequence. They did not make anybody uncomfortable except yourself."

"Cousin Kate," Candace ventured to ask, "will you tell me why there is such a thing as etiquette? Why must everybody eat and behave and speak in the same way, and make rules about it? Is it any real use?"

"That is rather a large question, and leads back to the beginning of things," said Mrs. Gray, smiling. "I don't suppose I quite understand it myself, but I think I can make you understand a part of it. I imagine, when the world was first peopled, in the strange faraway times of which we know almost nothing except the hints we get in the Bible, that the few people there were did pretty much as they liked. Noah and his family in the ark, for instance, probably never set any tables or had any regular meals, but just ate when they were hungry, each one by himself. Savage tribes do the same to this day; they seize their bone or their handful of meat and gnaw it in a corner, or as they walk about. This was the primitive idea of comfort. But after a time people found that it was less trouble to have the family food made ready at a certain time for everybody at once, and have all come together to eat it. Perhaps at first it was served in one great pot or dish, and each one dipped in his hand or spoon. The Arabs still do this. Then, of course, the strongest and greediest got the most of everything, and it may have been some weak or slow person who went hungry in consequence, who invented the idea of separate plates and portions."

"But that is not etiquette," objected Cannie. "People have plates and set tables everywhere now,—in this country, I mean."

"Yes, but can't you imagine a time when to have a bowl or a saucer to yourself was considered finical and 'stuck up,' and when some rough Frank or Gaul from the mountains looked on disapprovingly, and said that the world was coming to a pretty pass if such daintiness was to be allowed? A bowl to one's self was etiquette then. All sorts of things which to us seem matter of course and commonplace, began by being novelties and subjects for discussion and wonderment. Remember that tea, potatoes, carpets, tobacco, matches, almost all our modern conveniences, were quite unknown even so lately as four or five hundred years ago. As the world grew richer, people went on growing more refined. The richest folks tried to make their houses more beautiful than the houses of their neighbors. They gave splendid feasts, and hired sculptors and artists to invent decorations for their tables, and all kinds of little elegant usages sprang up which have gradually become the custom of our own day, even among people who are not rich and do not give feasts."

"But do they mean anything? Are they of any real use?" persisted Cannie.

"I confess that some of them do not seem to mean a great deal. Still, if we look closely, I think we shall find that almost every one had its origin in one of two causes,—either it was a help to personal convenience, or in some way it made people more agreeable or less disagreeable to their neighbors. We have to study, and to guess a little sometimes, to make out just why it has become customary to do this or that, for the original reason has been forgotten or perhaps does not exist any longer, while the custom remains."

"I wonder," said Cannie, whose mind was still running on her own mishaps, "why people mustn't cut fish with a steel knife. I read in a book once that it was not genteel to do so, and I couldn't think why. And then to-night I didn't see the little silver one—"

"I imagine that in the first instance some old gourmet discovered or fancied that a steel knife gave a taste to fish which injured it. So people gave up using knives, and it grew to be said that it was vulgar and a mark of ignorance to cut fish with them. Then, later, it was found not to be quite comfortable always to tear your bit of fish apart with a fork and hold it down with a piece of bread while you did so, and the custom arose of having a silver knife to cut fish with. It is a convenient custom, too, for some reasons. Waiting on table is quite an art, now-a-days, when there are so many changes of plates, and a good waiter always tries to simplify what he has to do, by providing as much as possible beforehand. You can see that if each person has beside his plate a silver knife for fish and a steel knife for meat and two forks these two courses will go on more easily and quietly than if the waiter has to stop and bring a fresh knife and fork for each person before he helps to the dish, whatever it is."

"But why is there nothing on the table but flowers and pretty little things? And why do they put lemon-peel in the bowls of water?"

"Well, the lemon is supposed to take the smell of dinner away from the fingers. And it isn't always lemon. Frederic is apt to drop in a geranium leaf or a sprig of lemon-verbena, and those are nicer. As for the other thing, it is more convenient for many reasons not to have the carving done on the table; but aside from that, I imagine that in the first instance the custom was a matter of economy."

"Economy!" repeated Candace, opening wide her eyes.

"Yes, economy, though it seems droll to say so. In the old days, when the meat came on in a big platter, and the vegetables each in its large covered dish, people had to put more on table than was really wanted, for the sake of not looking mean and giving their neighbors occasion for talk. Now, when everything is carved on a side-table and a nice little portion carried to each person, you are able to do with exactly what is needed. There need not be a great piece of everything left over for look's sake. One chicken is enough for four or five people if it is skilfully carved, but the chicken would look rather scanty on a platter by itself; don't you think so?"

"Yes," said Cannie, with a little laugh. She had forgotten her troubles in the interest of the discussion.

"A dish containing one mutton-chop and a spoonful of peas for each person would be called a stingy dish in the country, where every one sees his food on the table before him," continued Mrs. Gray; "but it is quite enough for the single course it is meant to be at a city dinner. There is no use in having three or four chops left over to toughen and grow cold."

"I see," said Cannie, thoughtfully; "what else did I do that was wrong, Cousin Kate?"

"You called Frederic 'sir,'" replied her cousin, with a smile. "That was not wrong, but not customary. Servants are expected to say 'sir' and 'ma'am' to their employers as a mark of respect; and people not servants use the word less frequently than they formerly did. They keep such terms for elderly or distinguished persons, to whom they wish to show special deference."

"But Aunt Myra always made me say 'sir' and 'ma'am' to her and grandpapa. She said it was impolite not to."

"She was quite right; for she and your grandfather were a great deal older than yourself, and it was only respectful to address them so. But you need not use the phrase to everybody to whom you speak."

"Not to you?"

"Well, I would quite as soon that in speaking to me you said, 'Yes, Cousin Kate,' as 'Yes, ma'am.' That is what I have taught my children to do. They say, 'Yes, mamma;' 'Did you call me, papa?' I like the sound of it better; but it is only a matter of taste. There is no real right or wrong involved in it."

Candace sat for a moment in silence, revolving these new ideas in her mind.

"Cousin Kate," she said timidly, "will you tell me when I make little mistakes, like that about the knife? I'd like to learn to do things right if I could, and if it wouldn't trouble you too much."

"Dear Cannie,"—and Mrs. Gray kissed her,—"I will, of course; and I am glad you like to have me. Your mother was the sweetest, most refined little lady that I ever knew. I loved her dearly; and I should love to treat you as I do my own girls, to whom I have to give a hint or a caution or a little lecture almost every day of their lives. No girl ever grew into a graceful, well-bred woman without many such small lessons from somebody. If your mother had lived, all these things would have come naturally to you from the mere fact of being with her and noticing what she did. You would have needed no help from any one else. But are you sure," she went on, after a little pause, "that you won't end by thinking me tiresome or interfering or worrisome, if I do as I say?"

"No, indeed, I won't!" cried Candace, to whom this long talk had been like the clearing up after a thunder-shower. "I think it would be too mean if I felt that way when you are so kind."

CHAPTER III.
A WALK ON THE CLIFFS.

IT is always an odd, unhomelike moment when one wakes up for the first time in a new place. Sleep is a separation between us and all that has gone before it. It takes a little while to recollect where we are and how we came there, and to get used to the strangeness which had partly worn away, but has come on again while we dreamed and forgot all about it.

Candace experienced this when she woke in the little blue room the morning after her arrival in Newport. She had gone to bed, by Mrs. Gray's advice, when their long talk about manners and customs was ended, and without going downstairs again.

"You are very tired, I can see," said Cousin Kate. "A long night's sleep will freshen you, and the world will look differently and a great deal pleasanter to-morrow."

Candace was glad to follow this counsel. She was tired, and she felt shy of Mr. Gray and the girls, and would rather put off meeting them again, she thought, till the morning. Ten hours of unbroken sleep rested her thoroughly, but she woke with a feeling of puzzled surprise at her surroundings, and for a few moments could not gather up her thoughts or quite recollect where she was. Then it all came back to her, and she was again conscious of the uncomfortable sensations of the night before.

She lay a little while thinking about it, and half wishing that she need not get up at all but just burrow under the blanket and hide herself, like a mouse or rabbit in his downy hole, till everybody had forgotten her blunders, and till she herself could forget them. But she said to herself bravely: "I won't be foolish. Cousin Kate is just lovely; she's promised to help me, and I'm sure she will. I will try not to mind the others; but, oh dear! I wish I were not so afraid of the girls."

She jumped out of bed resolutely and began to dress, taking her time about it, and stealing many glances out of the open window; for she knew it must be early, and as yet there were no sounds of life about the house. After her hair was curled, she stood for some time at the door of the closet, debating what dress she should put on.

The choice was limited. There were only a brown plaided gingham, a blue calico, and a thick white cambric to choose from. The latter seemed to her almost too nice to be worn in the morning. It was the first white dress she had ever been allowed to have, and Aunt Myra had said a good deal about the difficulty of getting it done up; so it seemed to Candace rather a sacred garment, which should be reserved for special state occasions.

After hesitating awhile she put on the brown gingham. It had a little ruffle basted round the neck. Candace tried the effect of a large blue bow, and then of a muslin one, very broad, with worked ends; but neither pleased her exactly. She recollected that Georgie and Gertrude had worn simple little ruches the night before, with no bows; and at last she wisely decided to fasten her ruffle with the little bar of silver which was her sole possession by way of ornament, for her mother's few trinkets had all been sold during her father's long illness. This pin had been a present from the worldly-minded Mrs. Buell, who so often furnished a text to Aunt Myra's homilies. She had one day heard Cannie say, when asked by one of the Buell daughters if she had any jewelry, "Are napkin-rings jewelry? I've got a napkin-ring." Mrs. Buell had laughed at the droll little speech, and repeated it as a good joke; but the next time she went to Hartford she bought the silver pin for Cannie, who was delighted, and held it as her choicest possession.

Her dressing finished, Candace went softly downstairs. She paused at the staircase window to look out. Cousin Kate's storm had not come after all. The day was brilliantly fair. Long fingers of sunshine were feeling their way through the tree-branches, seeking out shady corners and giving caressing touches to all growing things. A book lay on the window-bench. It was "A York and a Lancaster Rose," which little Marian had been reading the night before. It looked interesting, and, seeing by a glance at the tall clock in the hall below that it was but a little after seven, Candace settled herself for a long, comfortable reading before breakfast.

Mrs. Gray was the first of the family to appear. She swept rapidly downstairs in her pretty morning wrapper of pale pink, with a small muslin cap trimmed with ribbons of the same shade on her glossy black hair, and paused to give Cannie a rapid little kiss; but she looked preoccupied, and paid no further attention to her, beyond a kind word or two, till breakfast was over, the orders for the day given, half a dozen notes answered, and half a dozen persons seen on business. The girls seemed equally busy. Each had her own special little task to do. Georgie looked over the book-tables and writing-tables; sorted, tidied, put away the old newspapers; made sure that there was ink in the inkstands and pens and paper in plenty. After this was done, she set to work to water the plant boxes and stands in the hall and on the piazza. Gertrude fell upon a large box of freshly cut flowers, and began to arrange them in various bowls and vases. Little Marian had three cages of birds to attend to, which, as she was very particular about their baths and behavior, took a long time. Candace alone had nothing to do, and sat by, feeling idle and left out among the rest.

"I think I shall put you in charge of the piazza boxes," said Mrs. Gray, noticing her forlorn look as she came back from her interview with the fishmonger. "See, Cannie, the watering-pot is kept here, and the faucet of cold water is just there in the pantry. Would you like to take them as a little bit of daily regular work? They must be sprinkled every morning; and if the earth is dry they must be thoroughly watered, and all the seed-pods and yellow leaves and dead flowers must be picked off. Do you feel as if you could do it?"

"Oh, I should like to," said Cannie, brightening.

"Very well. Georgie has plenty to attend to without them, I imagine. She will be glad to be helped. Georgie, Cannie has agreed to take the care of all the outside flower-boxes in future. You needn't have them on your mind any more."

"That's nice," said Georgie, good-naturedly. "Then I will look after the plants on your balcony, mamma. Elizabeth doesn't half see to them."

"Oh, mightn't I do those too?" urged Cannie. "I wish you would let me."

"Well, you can if you like. They are all watered for to-day, though. You needn't begin till to-morrow."

"That is just as well," said Mrs. Gray; "for now that I am through with the orders and the tradesmen, I want Cannie to come up to the morning-room for a consultation. Georgie, you may come too. It's about your hair, Cannie. Those thick curls are very pretty, but they look a trifle old-fashioned, and I should think must be rather hot, like a little warm shawl always on your shoulders all summer long." She stroked the curls with her soft hand, as she spoke. "Should you dislike to have them knotted up, Cannie? You are quite old enough, I think."

"No, I shouldn't dislike it, but I don't know how to do my hair in any other way. I have always worn it like this."

"We'll teach you," cried Georgie and Gertrude, who had joined them while her mother was speaking. "Let us have a 'Council of Three' in the morning-room, and see what is most becoming to her."

So upstairs they went, and the girls pounced on Cannie, and put a towel over her shoulders, and brushed out her curls, and tried this way and that, while Mrs. Gray sat by and laughed. She would not interfere,—though Cannie at times resisted, and declared that they were pulling her hair and hurting her dreadfully,—for she was anxious that the cousins should grow intimate and familiar with each other. In fact, Cannie's shyness was quite shaken out of her for the moment; and before the experiments were ended, and it was decided that a little bang on the forehead, and what Marian called a "curly knot" behind, suited her best, she felt almost at home with Georgie and Gertrude.

"There," said Georgie, sticking in a last hair-pin, "come and see yourself; and if you don't confess that you are improved, you're a very ungrateful young person, and that is all I have to say."

Candace scarcely knew her own face when she was led up to the looking-glass. The light rings of hair lay very prettily on the forehead, the "curly knot" showed the shape of the small head; it all looked easy and natural, and as if it was meant to be so. She smiled involuntarily. The girl in the glass smiled back.

"Why, I look exactly like somebody else and not a bit like myself," she cried. "What would Aunt Myra say to me?"

"I am going out to do some errands," said Mrs. Gray; "will you come along, Cannie, and have a little drive?"

Mrs. Gray's errands seemed to be principally on behalf of her young companion. First they stopped at Seabury's, and after Mrs. Gray had selected a pair of "Newport ties" for herself, she ordered a similar pair for Candace. Then she said that while Cannie's shoe was off she might as well try on some boots, and Cannie found herself being fitted with a slender, shapely pair of black kid, which were not only prettier but more comfortable than the country-made ones which had made her foot look so clumsy. After that they stopped at a carpet and curtain place, where Cannie was much diverted at hearing the proprietor recommend tassels instead of plated rings on certain Holland shades, for the reason that "a tossel had more poetry about it somehow." Then, after a brief pause to order strawberries and fresh lettuce, the carriage was ordered to a milliner's.

"I want to get you a little hat of some sort," said Cousin Kate. "The one you wore yesterday is rather old for a girl of your age. I will retrim it some day, and it will do for picnics and sails, but you need more hats than one in this climate, which is fatal to ribbons and feathers, and takes the stiffness out of everything."

So a big, shady hat of dark red straw, with just a scarf of the same color twisted round the crown and a knowing little wing in front, was chosen; and then Mrs. Gray spied a smaller one of fine yellowish straw with a wreath of brown-centred daisies, and having popped it on Cannie's head for one moment, liked the effect, and ordered that too. Two new hats! It seemed to Cannie's modest ideas like the wildest extravagance; and after they returned to the coupé she found courage to say,—

"Cousin Kate, please, you mustn't buy me too many things."

"No, dear, I won't. I'll be careful," replied Mrs. Gray, smiling. Then, seeing that Cannie was in earnest, she added, more seriously: "My child, I've no wish to make you fine. I don't like finery for young girls; but one needs a good many things in a place like this, and I want to have you properly dressed in a simple way. It was agreed upon between Aunt Myra and myself that I should see to your summer wardrobe after you got here, because Newport is a better shopping-place than North Tolland; and while we are about it, we may as well get pretty things as ugly ones. It doesn't cost any more and is no more trouble, and I am sure you like them better, don't you?"

"Oh, yes, indeed," replied Cannie, quite relieved by this explanation. "I like pretty things ever so much—only—I thought—I was afraid—" She did not know how to finish her sentence.

The Old Stone Mill.
It was a roofless circular tower, supported on round arches.

"You were afraid I was ruining myself," asked her cousin, looking amused. "No, Cannie, I won't do that, I promise you; and in return, you will please let me just settle about a few little necessary things for you, just as I should for Georgie and Gertrude, and say no more about it. Ah! there is the old Mill; you will like to see that. Stop a moment, John."

The coupé stopped accordingly by a small open square, planted with grass and a few trees, and intersected with paths. There was a music-stand in the centre, a statue on a pedestal; and close by them, rising from the greensward, appeared a small, curious structure of stone. It was a roofless circular tower, supported on round arches, which made a series of openings about its base. Cannie had never heard of the Stone Mill before, and she listened eagerly while Mrs. Gray explained that it had stood there since the earliest days of the Colony; that no one knew exactly how old it was, who built it, or for what purpose it was built; and that antiquarians were at variance upon these points, and had made all sorts of guesses about its origin. Some insisted that it was erected by the Norsemen, who were the first to discover the New England shores, long before the days of Columbus; others supposed it to be a fragment of an ancient church. Others again—and Mrs. Gray supposed that these last were probably nearest the truth—insisted that it was just what it seemed to be, a mill for grinding corn; and pointed out the fact that mills of very much the same shape still exist in old country neighborhoods in England. She also told Cannie that the mill used to be thickly overhung with ivies and Virginia creepers, and that it had never been so pretty and picturesque since the town authorities, under a mistaken apprehension that the roots of the vines were injuring the masonry, had torn them all away and left the ruin bare and unornamented, as she now saw it.

"Did you never read Longfellow's 'Skeleton in Armor'?" she asked; and when Cannie said no, she repeated part of the poem, and promised to find the rest for Cannie to read when they got home. Then they drove on; and Cannie's head was so full of "Lief the son of Arnulf," the "fearful guest," and the maiden whose heart under her loosened vest fluttered like doves "in their nest frighted," that she could hardly bring herself back to real life, even when Cousin Kate stopped at a famous dress-furnisher's in the Casino Block, and caused her to be measured for two dresses. One was of white woollen stuff, like those which Georgie and Gertrude had worn the night before; the other, a darker one, of cream-and-brown foulard, which Mrs. Gray explained would be nice for church and for driving and for cool days, of which there were always plenty in the Newport summer. She also bought a little brown parasol for Cannie, and a tightly fitting brown jacket to match the foulard; and altogether it was a most exciting and adventurous morning. Cannie, as she took off her hat at home and fluffed the newly constructed "bang" into shape with gentle finger-touches, asked herself if it could be really only a day and a half since she said good-by to Aunt Myra in North Tolland; and if in fact it were really herself, little Candace Arden, to whom these wonderful things belonged, or was it some one else? Perhaps it was all a dream, and she should presently wake up. "If it be I, as I believe it be," was the tenor of her thought, as of the old woman in the nursery rhyme; only Cannie had no little dog at hand to help her to a realization of her own identity.

Into Candace's bare little cradle in the hill country had been dropped one precious endowment. From both her father and her mother she inherited the love of reading. If old tales were true, and the gift-conferring fairies really came to stand round a baby's bed, each with a present in her hand, I think out of all that they could bestow I should choose for any child in whom I was interested, these two things,—a quick sense of humor and a love for books. There is nothing so lasting or so satisfying. Riches may take wing, beauty fade, grace vanish into fat, a sweet voice become harsh, rheumatism may cripple the fingers which played or painted so deftly,—with each and all of these delightful things time may play sad tricks; but to life's end the power to see the droll side of events is an unfailing cheer, and so long as eyes and ears last, books furnish a world of interest and escape whose doors stand always open. Winds may blow and skies may rain, fortune may prove unkind, days may be lonely and evenings dull; but for the true lover of reading there is always at hand this great company of companions and friends,—the wisest, the gentlest, the best,—never too tired or too busy to talk with him, ready at all moments to give their thought, their teaching, to help, instruct, and entertain. They never disappoint, they have no moods or tempers, they are always at home,—in all of which respects they differ from the rest of our acquaintance. If the man who invented sleep is to be blessed, thrice blessed be the man who invented printing!

There were not many books in the old yellow farmhouse at North Tolland; but all that there were Cannie had read over and over again. Shakspeare she knew by heart, and "Paradise Lost," and Young's "Night Thoughts," and Pollock's "Course of Time." She had dipped into her dead father's theological library, and managed to extract some food for her imagination, even from such dry bones as "Paley's Evidences" and "Edwards on the Will and the Affections." Any book was better than no book to her. Aunt Myra, who discouraged the practice of reading for girls as unfitting them for any sort of useful work, used to declare that the very sight of a book made Cannie deaf and blind and dumb.

"You might as well be Laura what's-her-name and have done with it," she would tell her; "only I don't know where to look for a Dr. Howe or a Dr. anybody, who will come along and teach you to develop your faculties. I declare, I believe you'd rather read a dictionary any day than not read at all."

"I don't know but I would," said Cannie; but she said it to herself. She was rather afraid of Aunt Myra.

With this strong love of reading, the girl's delight may be imagined when Mrs. Gray, true to her promise, put into her hands a great illustrated volume of Longfellow, and left her free to dip and select and read as long as she chose. She curled herself up on the staircase bench, and was soon so deep in "The Skeleton in Armor" as to be quite oblivious to all that went on below. She did not hear the bell ring, she did not see various ladies shown into the drawing-room, or notice the hum of conversation that followed. She never lifted her eyes when Georgie Gray and a friend, who was no other than the identical Miss Joy of the "Eolus," stood at the staircase foot for some moments and held a whispered conversation; nor was she conscious of the side glances which the visitor now and then cast up toward the brown gingham skirt visible above. It was not till

"Skoal! to the Northland! skoal!"

ended the poem, that her dream ended, and she roused herself to find the callers gone and luncheon on the table.

Mrs. Gray was wont to say that they always had a meal at noon and a meal at night; and when her husband was at home, the first was called lunch and the second dinner, and when he was away the first was called dinner and the second supper; and that the principal difference between them was that at one there was soup and at the other there was not. Candace did not particularly care what the meal was called. Under any name she was glad of it, for sea-air and a morning drive had made her very hungry; and this time she was on her guard, watched carefully what others did, and made no serious blunders.

"What are you girls going to do this afternoon?" asked Mrs. Gray.

"Berry Joy has asked me to drive with her," replied Georgie; "she wants to take her friend over to the Fort to hear the band play. You have no objection, have you, mamma?"

"No; none at all. And you, Gertrude?"

"I haven't made any particular plan."

"Then suppose you and Candace take a walk on the Cliffs. I have to take Marian to the dentist; but Cannie has not seen the sea yet, except at a distance, and you both ought to have a good exercise in the fresh air, for I am almost sure it will rain by to-morrow. You might take her to the beach, Gertrude, and come home by Marine Avenue."

"Very well, mamma; I will, certainly," said Gertrude. But there was a lack of heartiness in her tone. Like most very young girls she had a strong sense of the observant eyes of Mrs. Grundy, and she did not at all approve of the brown gingham. "I wonder why mamma can't wait till she has made Cannie look like other people," she was saying to herself.

There was no help for it, however. None of Mrs. Gray's children ever thought of disputing her arrangements for a moment; so the two girls set forth, Cannie in the despised gingham, and Gertrude in a closely fitting suit of blue serge, with a large hat of the same blue, which stood out like a frame round the delicate oval of her face, and set off the feathery light hair to perfection.

Their way for a little distance was down a sort of country lane, which was the short cut to the Cliffs. It ended in a smooth greensward at the top of a wall of broken rocks; and, standing on the edge, Cannie called out, "Oh!" with a sense of sudden surprise and freedom.

Before her was a bay of the softest blue, with here and there a line of white surf, where long rollers were sweeping in toward the distant beach. Opposite, stretched a point of land rising into a low hill, which shone in the yellow afternoon sun; and from its end the unbroken sea stretched away into a lovely distance, whose color was like that of an opal, and which had no boundary but a mysterious dim line of faintly tinted sky. Sails shone against the moving water; gulls were dipping and diving; a flock of wild-ducks with glossy black heads swam a little away out from the shore.

Beyond the point which made the other arm of the little bay rose an island, ramparted by rocks, over which the surf could be seen to break with an occasional toss of spray. There was a delicious smell of soft salty freshness, and something besides,—a kind of perfume which Candace could not understand or name.

"Oh, what is it; what can it be?" she said.

"What?"

"The smell. It is like flowers. Oh, there it is again!"

"Mamma makes believe that it is the Spice Islands," answered Gertrude, indifferently, "or else Madeira. You know there is nothing between us and the coast of Africa except islands."

"Really and truly? How wonderful!"

"Well, I don't see how it is so very wonderful. It just happens so. I suppose there are plenty of sea-side places where they can say the same thing."

"Perhaps,—but I never saw any sea-coast but this. It is all new to me."

"I suppose so," responded Gertrude, with a little yawn. She looked to right and to left, fearing that some acquaintance might be coming to see her in company with this rather shabby little companion. "Would you like to walk up the Cliffs a little way, or shall we go down to the beach?" she asked.

"Oh, let us just go as far as that point," said Candace, indicating where, to the right, past a turnstile, a smooth gravel path wound its way between the beautifully kept borders of grass. The path ran on the very edge of the Cliff, and the outer turf dipped at a steep incline to where the sharp rock ran down perpendicularly, but to the very verge it was as fine and as perfectly cut as anywhere else. Candace wondered who held the gardeners and kept them safe while they shaved the grass so smoothly in this dangerous spot, but she did not like to ask. Gertrude's indifferent manner drove her in upon herself and made her shy.

A hundred feet and more below them the sea was washing into innumerable rocky fissures with a hollow booming sound. The cliff-line was broken into all sorts of bold forms,—buttresses and parapets and sharp inclines, with here and there a shallow cave or a bit of shingly beach. Every moment the color of the water seemed to change, and the soft duns and purples of the horizon line to grow more intense. Candace had no eyes but for the sea. She scarcely noticed the handsome houses on her right hand, each standing in its wide lawn, with shrubberies and beds of dazzling flowers. Gertrude, on the contrary, scarcely looked at the sea. It was an old story to her; and she was much more interested in trying to make out people she knew at the windows of the houses they passed, or on their piazzas, and in speculating about the carriages which could be seen moving on the distant road.

"How good it is of the people who own the places to let everybody go through them!" exclaimed Candace, when it was explained to her that the Cliff walk was a public one.

"Oh, they can't help themselves. There is a right of way all round the Island, and nobody would be allowed to close it. Some owners grumble and don't like it a bit; but mamma says it is one of the best things in Newport, and that it would be a great injury to the place to have it taken away. The Cliff walk is very celebrated, you know. Lots of people have written things about it."

"Oh, I should think they would. It is the most beautiful place I ever saw."

"You haven't seen many places, have you?" observed Gertrude, rather impolitely.

"Oh no, I never saw anything but North Tolland till I came to Newport."

"Then you can't judge."

They had now turned, and were walking eastward toward the beach. Its line of breaking surf could be distinctly seen now. Carriages and people on horseback were driving or riding along the sands, and groups of black dots were discernible, which were other people on foot.

"There is Pulpit Rock," said Gertrude, stopping where a shelving path slanted down toward a great square mass of stone, which was surrounded on three sides by water. "Would you like to go down and sit on top for a little while? I am rather tired."

"Oh, I should like to so much."

Down they scrambled accordingly, and in another moment were on top of the big rock. It was almost as good as being at sea; for when they turned their backs to the shore nothing could be seen but water and sails and flying birds, and nothing heard but the incessant plash and dash of the waves below.

"Oh, how perfectly splendid!" cried Cannie. "I should think you would come here every day, Gertrude."

"Yes, that's what people always say when they first come," said the experienced Gertrude. "But I assure you we don't come every day, and we don't want to. Why, sometimes last summer I didn't see the Cliffs for weeks and weeks together. It's nice enough now when there are not many people here; but after the season begins and the crowd, it isn't nice at all. You see all sorts of people that you don't know, and—and—well—it isn't pleasant."

"I can't think what you mean," declared Cannie, opening her eyes with amazement. "I'd just as soon there were twenty people on this rock, if I needn't look at them and they didn't talk to me. The sea would be just the same."

"You'll feel differently when you've been in Newport awhile. It's not at all the fashion to walk on the Cliffs now except on Sunday, and not at this end of them even then. A great many people won't bathe, either,—they say it has grown so common. Why, it used to be the thing to walk down here,—all the nicest people did it; and now you never see anybody below Narragansett Avenue except ladies'-maids and butlers, and people who are boarding at the hotels and don't know any better."

"How funny it seems!" remarked Candace, half to herself, with her eyes on the distance, which was rapidly closing in with mist.

"What is funny?"

"Oh, I was—I was only thinking how funny it is that there should be a fashion about coming down to such a beautiful place as this."

"I don't see how it is funny."

"Yes," persisted Candace, who, for all her shyness, had ideas and opinions of her own; "because the Cliffs are so old and have always been here, and I suppose some of the people who make it the fashion not to walk upon them have only just come to Newport."

"I really think you are the queerest girl I ever saw," said Gertrude.

A long silence ensued. Each of the two girls was thinking her own thoughts. The thickening on the horizon meanwhile was increasing. Thin films of vapor began to blow across the sky. The wind stirred and grew chill; the surf on the beach broke with a low roar which had a menacing sound. Suddenly a wall of mist rose and rolled rapidly inland, blotting out all the blue and the smile of sky and sea.

"Gracious! here's the fog," cried Gertrude, "and I do believe it's going to rain. We must hurry home. I rather think mamma's storm is coming, after all."

CHAPTER IV.
THE MANUAL OF PERFECT GENTILITY.

MRS. GRAY'S storm had indeed come. All the next day it rained, and the day after it rained harder, and on the third day came a thick fog; so it was not till the very end of the week that Newport lay again in clear sunshine.

The first of the wet days Cannie spent happily in the society of Miss Evangeline and Mr. Hiawatha, two new acquaintances of whom she felt that she could scarcely see enough. Marian found her sitting absorbed on the staircase bench, and after peeping over her shoulder at the pictures for a while, begged her to read aloud. It was the first little bit of familiar acquaintance which any of the younger members of the Gray family had volunteered, and Candace was much pleased.

Marian was not yet quite fourteen, and was still very much of a child at heart and in her ways. Her "capable" little face did not belie her character. She was a born housekeeper, always tidying up and putting away after other people. Everything she attempted she did exactly and well. She was never so happy as when she was allowed to go into the kitchen to make molasses candy or try her hand at cake; and her cake was almost always good, and her candy "pulled" to admiration. She was an affectionate child, with a quick sense of fun, and a droll little coaxing manner, which usually won for her her own way, especially from her father, who delighted in her and never could resist Marian's saucy, caressing appeals. It required all Mrs. Gray's firm, judicious discipline to keep her from being spoiled.

Georgie, who was nearly nineteen, seemed younger in some respects than Gertrude, who was but three months older than Candace. Georgie, too, had a good deal of the housekeeper's instinct, but she was rather dreamy and puzzle-headed, and with the best intentions in the world was often led into scrapes and difficulties from her lack of self-reliance, and the easy temper which enabled any one who was much with her to gain an influence over her mind.

Gertrude—but it is less easy to tell what Gertrude was. In fact, it was less important just then to find out what she was than what she was likely to be. Gertrude reminded one of an unripe fruit. The capacities for sweetness and delightfulness were there within her, but all in a crude, undeveloped state. No one could predict as yet whether she would ripen and become mellow and pleasant with time, or remain always half-hard and half-sour, as some fruits do. Meanwhile she was the prettiest though not the most popular of the Gray sisters, and she ruled over Georgie's opinions and ideas with the power which a stronger and more selfish character always has over a weaker and more pliable one.

Marian was less easily influenced. She and Gertrude often came into collision; and it was in part the habit of disputing Gertrude's mandates which led her to seek out Candace on that rainy afternoon. In the privacy of her own room that morning, Gertrude had made some very unflattering remarks about their newly arrived relative.

"It's really quite dreadful to have a girl like that come to spend the whole summer with one," she said to Georgie. "She hasn't a bit of style, and her clothes are so queer and old-timey; and she's always lived up on that horrid farm, and hasn't an idea beyond it. Everything surprises her so, and she makes such a fuss over it. You should have heard her yesterday when we were out walking; she said the Cliffs had been there always, and some of the fashionable people had only just come."

"What did she mean?"

"I'm sure I don't know. She says the queerest things. And she looks so funny and so different from the other girls; and of course everybody will know that she is our cousin."

"Mamma has ordered her some dresses from Hollander's," observed Georgie; "and that was a real pretty hat that came home last night."

"I don't care. They won't look like anything when she puts them on."

"Gertrude Gray, I think it's real mean to talk so about your own cousin," cried Marian, who, with the instinct of a

68

true "little pitcher," had heard every word. "It isn't Cannie's fault that she has always lived on a farm. She didn't have anywhere else to live. Very likely she would have preferred Paris," with fine scorn, "or to go to boarding-school in Dresden, as you and Georgie did, if anybody had given her the choice. She's real nice, I think, and now that her hair is put up, she's pretty too,—a great deal prettier than some of the girls you like. I'm going down now to sit with her. You and Georgie don't treat her kindly a bit. You leave her all alone, and very likely she's homesick at this moment; but I shall be nice to her, whatever you do."

Whereupon Miss Marian marched out of the room with her nose in the air, and devoted herself to Candace for the rest of that day, much to the lonely little visitor's contentment.

They grew quite at home with each other over "Evangeline." Birthday books had just come into fashion. Somebody had given Marian one; and she now brought it and asked Candace to write in it.

"June 17," she said, as Cannie sought out the right page; "why, that is next Saturday."

"So it is, though I shouldn't have remembered it if it hadn't been for your book."

"Why, how funny!" cried Marian, opening her eyes wide. "Don't you keep your birthdays?"

"Keep them?" repeated Candace, in a tone of perplexity.

"Yes; keep—celebrate them? Don't people ever give you presents? Didn't you ever have a cake?"—her voice increasing in dismay, as Candace in answer to each question shook her head.

"Cake—on my birthday, you mean? No, I don't think I ever did. Aunt Myra doesn't believe in cake. She says she liked it when she was young; but since she was converted to cracked wheat and oatmeal at the age of thirty-three, she has hardly ever touched it. We never had any at North Tolland, except gingerbread sometimes."

"What a dreadful kind of aunt for a girl to have!" remarked Marian, meditatively. She sat for some time longer on the floor, with her head on Candace's knee; but she seemed to be thinking deeply about something, and said she didn't feel like being read to any longer. At last she went away "to speak to mamma," she said.

Candace had forgotten all about this birthday discussion before Saturday morning dawned dimly out of the still persistent fog. All the time she was dressing, her eyes were on "The Golden Legend" which lay open on the bureau beside her; and her thoughts were so much occupied with Prince Henry and poor pretty Elsie, for whom she felt so very sorry, that she had none to spare for the comparatively unimportant fact that she, little Candace Arden, had that day turned the corner of her seventeenth year.

It was all the more a delightful surprise, therefore, when she went down to breakfast and found a pile of dainty, white, ribbon-tied parcels on her plate, a glass of beautiful roses beside it, and was met with a special kiss from Cousin Kate, and a chorus of "Many happy returns" from the rest of the family.

The little softnesses and prettinesses of life, the gifts and surprises, the sweet words, the being made much of on special occasions, were quite unknown to the old farm-house in North Tolland. Aunt Myra was a stanch Presbyterian. She disapproved on principle of Christmas day, as belonging to popery and old superstition. She didn't see that one day was any better than any other day. It was just an accident on what day of the year you were born, and it was no use to make a fuss about it, she said. There were plenty of people in the world before you came, and there would have been plenty if you had never come at all. Such was Aunt Myra's dictum.

With these views, it may be supposed that Candace's idea of an anniversary was not a very lively one. For a moment she scarcely took in the meaning of what she saw, but stood regarding the plate-ful of parcels with a bewildered look on her face.

"It's your birthday, you know," exclaimed little Marian. "Many happy returns! Don't you recollect that it's your birthday? We shouldn't have found it out, though, if it hadn't been for my book."

"I'm not so sure about that," said Mrs. Gray, smiling at her. "I had the date of Cannie's birthday put down securely somewhere, and I've been keeping a special gift for it. It's something that I brought you from Geneva, Cannie; but as it had waited so long before getting to you, I thought it might as well wait a little longer and come on your anniversary."

"Oh, thank you," said Candace, glancing shyly at the parcels.

"Please do begin to open them!" urged Marian. "It is such fun to see people open presents. That's mamma's; open it first."

It was a flat squarish bundle, tied with a rose-colored ribbon. Cannie's fingers shook with excitement as she undid the knot. Breakfast meantime was at a stand-still. The girls were peeping over her shoulders, Mr. Gray watching from behind his newspaper; even Frederic, with a plate of hot toast in his hand, had paused, and out of one discreet eye was observing her movements.

Inside was a flat case of gray polished wood, with a little silver ornament in the middle. It opened with a snap. Cannie pressed the spring, the lid flew up, and there, on a cushion of blue velvet, lay the prettiest little Swiss watch imaginable, with C. V. A. enamelled on its lid. There was a slender gold chain attached, a little enamelled key,—nothing could be more complete.

"A watch! for me! to be my own!" cried Candace, hardly able to believe her eyes. "I never thought I should have a watch, and such a darling beauty as this. Oh, Cousin Kate!"

"I am glad it pleases you," said her cousin, with another kiss. "You should have had it two years ago; but I thought you rather young to be trusted with a watch then, so I kept it till we should meet."

"Oh, do make haste and open another! It's such fun to see you," pleaded Marian.

One by one, the other parcels were unfastened. There was a little ring of twisted gold from Georgie, a sachet of braided ribbons, dark and light blue, from Gertrude, a slender silver bangle from Marian, and from Mr. Gray a long roll of tissue paper in which lay six pairs of undressed kid gloves in pretty shades of tan color and pale yellow. There was besides a big box of candy. This, Mr. Gray declared, was his real present. Cousin Kate was responsible for the gloves, but he knew very well that there never yet was a girl of seventeen who did not have a sweet tooth ready for a sugar-plum.

One bundle remained. It was tied with pink packthread instead of ribbon. Cannie undid the string. It was a book, not new, bound in faded brown; and the title printed on the back was "The Ladies' Manual of Perfect Gentility."

"Who on earth gave you that?" demanded Marian.

Mrs. Gray looked surprised and not very well pleased.

"It is a joke, I suppose," she said. "Georgie, Gertrude,— which of you has been amusing yourself in this odd way?"

"Not I, mamma," said Georgie. Gertrude felt the reproof in her mother's manner, but she tried to laugh the matter off.

"Oh, I put it there just for fun," she said. "I thought the more parcels the better, and I happened to see that queer old thing, and thought it would make Cannie laugh."

This explanation was not quite sincere. Gertrude had put the book on the table, hoping to tease Cannie. She had overheard something which her mother was telling Candace the day before,—an explanation about some little point of manners,—and it had suggested the idea of the old volume. Her shaft had missed its mark somehow, or, like the boomerangs used by the Australian blacks, had returned again to the hand that aimed it; for Cannie did not seem to mind at all, and Mrs. Gray, though she said no more at the moment, was evidently meditating a lecture. It came after breakfast, and was unexpectedly severe, hurting Gertrude a great deal more than her maliciously intended gift had hurt Candace.

"You are inclined to despise your cousin as countrified and unused to society," said Mrs. Gray. "I grant that she is not up in all the little social rules; but let me tell you, Gertrude, that Cannie has the true instinct of ladyhood in her, and after the occurrence of this morning I am beginning to fear that you have not. Good manners are based on good feeling. Cannie may be shy and awkward; she may not know how to face a room full of strangers gracefully,—such things are not hard to learn, and she will learn them in time; but of one thing I am very sure, and that is, that if you were her guest at North Tolland instead of her being yours at Newport, she would be quite incapable of any rudeness however slight, or of trying to make you uncomfortable in any way. I wish I could say the same of you, Gertrude. I am disappointed in you, my child."

"Oh, mamma, don't speak so!" cried Gertrude, almost ready to cry; for she admired her mother as well as loved her, and was cravingly desirous to win her good opinion. "Please don't think I meant to be rude. It really and truly was a joke."

"My dear, you meant a little more by it than that," replied Mrs. Gray, fixing her soft, penetrating look on Gertrude's face. "You haven't begun quite rightly with Candace. I have noticed it, and have been sorry,—sorry for you even more than for her. She is an affectionate, true-hearted girl. You can make a good friend of her if you will; and you can be of use to her and she to you."

"Now, what did mamma mean by that?" thought Gertrude, after she had gone upstairs. "I can't, for the life of me, see what use Cannie could be to me. I might to her, perhaps, if I wanted to."

The "Manual of Perfect Gentility" was destined to excite more attention than its donor had intended, in more ways than one. Candace and Marian fell to reading it, and found its contents so amusing that they carried it to the morning-room, where Georgie was taking a lesson in china-painting from her mother, who was very clever at all the minor art accomplishments. Gertrude came in at the same time, in search of some crewels to match an embroidery pattern; so they were all together.

"Mamma, mamma, please listen to this!" cried Marian, and she read:—

"'Directions for entering the room at an evening party.—Fix your eye on the lady of the house on entering, and advance toward her with outstretched hand, looking neither to the right nor to the left, until you have interchanged the ordinary salutations of the occasion. When this is done, turn aside and mingle with the other guests.'

Now, mamma, just imagine it,—marching in with your hand out and your eye fixed!" And Marian, relinquishing the Manual to Cannie, flew to the door, and entered in the manner prescribed, with her eyes set in a stony glare on her mother's face, and her hand held before her as stiffly as if it had been a shingle. No one could help laughing.

"I don't think the hand and the glare are necessary," said Mrs. Gray; "but it is certainly quite proper to speak to the lady of the house, when you come in, before you begin to talk to other people."

"Here's another," cried Marian, hardly waiting till her mother had done speaking. "Just listen to these—

"'Directions for a horseback ride. Mounting.—The lady should stand on the left side of the horse, with her right hand on the pommel of her saddle, and rest her left foot lightly on the shoulder of her gentleman attendant, who bends before her. When this is done, the gentleman will slowly raise himself to the perpendicular position, and in doing so lift the lady without difficulty to the level of her seat.'"

"My gracious! suppose he didn't," remarked Georgie, looking up from her painting. "There she would be, standing on his shoulder, on one foot! Imagine it, on the Avenue!" And the four girls united in a peal of laughter.

"But there is something here that I really want to know about," said Candace. "May I read it to you, Cousin Kate? It's in a chapter called 'Correspondence.'"

"Oh, my!" cried Marian, who still held fast to one side of the Manual. "It tells how to refuse gentlemen when they offer themselves to you. Here it all is. You must say,—

"'Sir,—I regret extremely if anything in my manner has led to a misapprehension of my true feelings. I do not experience for you the affection which alone can make the marriage relation a happy one; so I—'"

"No, no," interrupted Candace, blushing very pink, and pulling the book away from Marian; "that isn't at all what I wanted to ask you about, Cousin Kate. It was—"

"Oh, then perhaps you meant to accept him," went on the incorrigible Marian, again getting possession of one side of the "Manual of Gentility." "Here you are:—

"'Dear Friend,—Your letter has made me truly happy, breathing, as it does, expressions of deep and heartfelt affection, of which I have long felt the corresponding sentiments. I shall be happy to receive you in my home as an accepted suitor, and I—'"

"Cousin Kate, make her stop—isn't she too bad?" said Cannie, vainly struggling for the possession of the book.

"'And I'—let me see, where was I when you interrupted?" went on Marian. "Oh, yes, here—

"'And I am sure that my parents will give their hearty consent to our union. Receive my thanks for your assurances, and believe—'"

But Candace had again got hold of the volume, and no one ever learned the end of the letter, or what the lover of this obliging lady was to "believe."

"This is what I wanted to ask you about, Cousin Kate," said Candace, when quiet was restored. "The book says:—

"'The signature of a letter should depend upon the degree of familiarity existing between the writer and the person addressed. For instance, in writing to a perfect stranger a lady would naturally use the form,—

Yours truly,
Mrs. A. M. Cotterell.'"

"Oh! oh!" interrupted Georgie. "Fancy any one signing herself 'Yours truly, Mrs. A. M. Cotterell.' It's awfully vulgar, isn't it mamma?"

"That is a very old-fashioned book," observed Mrs. Gray; "still I don't think, even at the time when it was published, that well-bred people used a signature like that. It may not be 'awfully vulgar,' but it certainly is not correct; nothing but the Christian name should ever be used as a signature."

"But suppose the person you were writing to did not know whether you were married or not," said Candace.

"Then you can add your address below, like this;" and she wrote on the edge of her drawing-paper,—

"Yours truly,
"Catherine V. Gray.

"Mrs. Courtenay Gray,
"Newport, R. I.

That is what I should do if I were writing to a stranger."

"Then there is this about the addresses of letters," went on Candace:—

"'In addressing a married lady, use her maiden as well as her married name; for example, in writing to Miss Sarah J. Beebe, who is married to George Gordon, the proper direction would be

Mrs. Sarah B. Gordon,
Care of George Gordon,
Oshkosh,
Michigan.'

Is that right, Cousin Kate?"

"No; that is decidedly wrong. When Miss Beebe married, she became not only Mrs. Gordon, but Mrs. George Gordon, to distinguish her from any other Mrs. Gordons who might happen to exist. She should sign herself 'Sarah B. Gordon,' but her letters and cards should bear her married name, 'Mrs. George Gordon.'"

"But people do write to widows in that way, don't they?" asked Gertrude. "I recollect, when I went to the post-office with Berry Joy one day, there was a letter for her mother, directed to Mrs. Louisa Bailey Joy."

"Yes; people do, but not the people who know the right way," her mother replied dryly. "A man's Christian name doesn't die with him any more than his surname. I often see letters addressed to Mrs. Jane this and Mrs. Maria that, but it never seems to me either correct or elegant. It is a purely

American custom. English people have never adopted it, and it seems very odd to them."

"Well, about cards," continued Marian, who was turning over the leaves of the "Manual of Gentility." "See what a funny little card this is; and the writer of the book says it is the kind we ought to have." She pointed to a page on which appeared a little oblong enclosure bearing the name

Fannie C. Jones.

"That isn't nice a bit, is it, mamma?"

"No, I confess that it does not look to me at all right. Girls old enough to need cards are old enough to have 'handles to their names.' If I were that young woman I should spell 'Fanny' without the ie, and call myself 'Miss Frances C. Jones' on my card, and keep my pet name for the use of my friends, and not print it."

"I think I've learned a good deal to-day," said Candace. "The funny old book isn't right in what it says, but Cousin Kate knows; so it comes to the same thing in the end. I'm glad you gave it to me, Gertrude."

Gertrude had the grace to feel ashamed, as she saw Candace's perfect freedom from shame.

"Oh, dear! how much there is to learn!" continued Candace, with a sigh. She was still deep in the "Ladies' Manual of Perfect Gentility."

"Put away that book, Cannie," said her cousin; "or give it to me, and I will hide it where Gertrude shall not find it again. Good breeding can be learned without printed rules."

"Can it, mamma?"

"Yes; for, as I was saying this morning to Gertrude, good manners are the result of good feeling. If we really care about other people, and want to make them happy, and think of them and not of ourselves, we shall instinctively do what will seem pleasant to them, and avoid doing what is disagreeable. We shall refrain from interrupting them when they are speaking. We shall not half listen to what they say, while our eyes are roving about the room, and our attention wandering to other things. We shall be quick to notice if they want anything that we can get for them. We shall not answer at random, or giggle, or say the wrong thing. We shall not loll back in our chairs, as Georgie is doing at this moment, with one foot cocked over the other knee, and a paint-brush in our mouths."

"Mamma!" And Georgie hastily recovered the upright position, and took her paint-brush from between her lips.

"We shall not drum idly on window-panes, as Gertrude was doing just now, for fear that the little noise will be disagreeable to our neighbors."

"Now, mamma!"

"We shall not walk carelessly between any one and the fire, because we shall be afraid of making them cold; nor shall we upset a work-basket while doing so, as Marian upset mine just now."

"Mamma, I do believe you are giving us all a scolding; I shall just stop you." And Marian flung her arms round her mother's neck, and gave her half a dozen enormous kisses.

"We shall consider a kiss as a favor," went on Mrs. Gray, inexorably, holding Marian off at arm's length, "not a punishment to be inflicted whenever we happen to feel like it. We shall never trot one foot when we are nervous, and shake the table."

"Cannie, that's you. I thought it would be your turn soon," said Marian.

"Oh! did I trot?" said Cannie. "Please excuse me, Cousin Kate. I have such a bad habit of doing that. Aunt Myra says it's my safety-valve."

"If it's a safety-valve, it's all very well," replied her cousin. "I didn't know. In short, my dears, as the poet says,—

'Manners are not idle, but the fruit
Of noble nature and of lofty mind.'

The instinct of self-control, of gentleness, of consideration and forethought and quick sympathy, which go to make up what we call good breeding; the absence of noise and hurry, the thousand and one little ways by which we can please people, or avoid displeasing them,—are all taught us by our own hearts. Good manners are the fine flower of civilization. And everybody can have them. I always say that one of the best-bred men of my acquaintance is Mr. Jarvis, the mason. I have known him come up out of a cistern to speak to me, dressed in overalls and a flannel shirt; and his bow and his manner and the politeness of his address would have done credit to any gentleman in the world."

"Mamma, how funny you are," said Georgie, wonderingly; but Gertrude caught her mother's meaning more clearly.

"I rather like it," she said slowly. "It sounds like something in a poem or a storybook, and it would be nice if everybody felt like that, but people don't. I've heard Mrs. Joy speak quite rudely to Mr. Jarvis, mamma."

"Very likely. I never have considered Mrs. Joy as a model of manners," replied Mrs. Gray, coolly. "And that reminds me to say just one other word about good breeding toward servants and people who work for us, or are poor and need our help. Gentleness and politeness are even more important with them than they are with other people."

"Why more, mamma?"

"Because their lives are harder than ours, and we owe them all the little help that courtesy can give. Because, too, we are their models, consciously or unconsciously, and if we are polite to them they will in return be polite to us. And besides, they meet us at a disadvantage. If a servant 'answers back,' she is called impertinent and discharged; but I should think it must be rather hard not to answer back to some mistresses."

"Is that why you are always so very polite to Jane?" asked Gertrude. Jane was the cook.

"Yes, partly that; and partly because I want Jane to be very polite to me; and she always is."

"There is the sun at last, I do declare," cried Marian, springing up. "Hurrah! I should think it was time. Now we shall have some nice weather, Cannie. Newport is lovely after a fog. It looks so nicely washed, and so green. Mamma, couldn't we have a long drive this afternoon in the wagonette, across the beaches and way round by the windmill? I like that drive so much."

"Yes; and at dinner we will eat Cannie's health in her birthday cake. It is making now, and Jane has the seventeen little pink candles all ready. How the fog is rolling away! It will be a charming afternoon."

CHAPTER V.
DOWN TO BEAVER TAIL.

SUNDAY morning brought the fresh, lovely stillness which Sundays in early summer seem always to possess in Newport. Later in the season the roll of wheels and the jingle of plated harnesses come to mar this peacefulness; but till the very end of June it endures, and is one of the sweet things of the place.

The Joys were at breakfast. It was one of the points in which Mrs. Joy took most pride, that this meal was served in a special apartment known as the breakfast-room, and not, as with most families, in the room where they dined. The breakfast-room was not large, but sumptuous in all its appointments. A critical taste might have objected that the plush curtains which shaded the windows were too heavy for summer; that the begilded wallpaper "swore" a little at its own dado and frieze, as well as deadened the effect of the pictures which hung against it; and that the drapery of lace and velvet which veiled the fireplace made a fire inconvenient and almost impossible, however cold the weather might be. But a critical taste might have found the same faults with the whole house. The general effect was of costliness and magnificence; but the details were at variance, and comfort and homelikeness had been sacrificed in the effort to make everything fine. There was a library, with almost no books in it; a ball-room, which was used only for balls, and looked bare and shut up on ordinary days; a huge drawing-room, full of costly toys,—tables loaded with Sèvres cups, other tables with processions of pug-dogs in precious china, snuff-boxes, patch-boxes; chimney-piece crowded with porcelain figures and bits of old Dresden ware; there was a great deal of carving and or-moulu,—but it all had the air of being created and kept for company use, and deserted the moment company went away. Mrs. Joy had only got so far in her art education as this, that she bought everything which cost a great deal of money and which her neighbors bought, and she never stopped to reason about such minor points as taste, fitness, convenience, or the adaptation of an article to her own particular needs.

Mrs. Joy was the very image of a prosperous woman, as she sat behind her heavy silver coffee-pots and cream-jugs, reading the Sunday paper, to get which her groom had ridden a couple of miles before breakfast. Her very black hair was trained into a line of formal rings across her forehead, which as yet scarcely showed a wrinkle. Her tightly laced figure was almost as slender as her daughter's; and the hand sparkling with diamonds, which held the paper, was white and youthful. Handsome she certainly was; and people called her agreeable, for she talked a great deal, in a noisy, lively way, and had a caressing manner for all persons whom she thought it worth her while to caress. But her face was hard; and when the society smile died out of it, it was neither intelligent nor kindly. Mrs. Joy had been extremely pretty in her youth. Berenice was like her; but Tom Joy the son resembled his father, who had died three or four years before the opening of this little story.

Berry and her friend Ethel Curtis were talking about a sailing party which they had planned for the next day.

"The Grays and the Halletts, and Julia Prime, that makes seven; mamma for matron, eight; then there's Tom and George Rivington, and the two Fosters. I can't think where we are to get the other three men."

"It isn't like a dinner party. The numbers need not be exactly equal," suggested Ethel.

"That's true, but it's a great deal better fun to have them equal. Men hate to talk to two girls at once, and the girls who haven't any men to talk to feel left out. Carrol Benton is coming up the end of the week; I wish he were here now."

"I guess you'd better look up some other matron, and let me off," said Mrs. Joy, laying down her newspaper. "I don't care much for sailing. I'm so apt to feel a little sick, and that spoils all the pleasure of it. Ask Mrs. Freddy Allen; she is young, and likes to go everywhere, and Freddy will go along and make another gentleman."

"That will do nicely if you really don't want to go, mamma. We'll invite them all as we come out of church, and save the bother of writing notes. It's easier to explain when you see people than to write down everything."

"Yes, that's one of the conveniences of going to church," remarked Mrs. Joy, calmly. "I've often had as many as three or four invitations, coming out of Trinity on a Sunday morning in the season. These muffins are horrid. James, tell the cook she ought to be ashamed of herself to send up such things. They're as tough as leather, and burned besides—as black as my shoe, I do declare."

"Yes, 'm."

And James departed to incense the cook with the unsoftened message. The cook declared that when ladies came down an hour late for breakfast, they must expect tough muffins; and for her part she didn't care whether they were good or not; she didn't think much of the place anyway, and didn't mean to stay on. There'd be plenty of people coming in a week or two, and plenty of places to pick and choose from. Mrs. Joy was always having little difficulties with her servants.

Trinity Church looked cool and shady, as the party entered it from the dazzle of the outer sunshine. Berenice Joy was perfectly well-trained in the outward forms of devotion. She called herself "High Church;" and nothing could be more graceful than the manner in which she glided up the aisle, bowed to the chancel, and sank on her knees, for what was supposed to be a short interval of silent prayer. But her eyes went straight to the Grays' pew the moment she rose, and from thence to the Halletts', and she whispered to Ethel, "They're all here. That's nice." Then she indulged in a long stare at Candace, who had come to church with her cousins, and who, in her new cream-and-brown foulard, with the daisy-trimmed hat, and a pair of the birthday gloves on her slender hands, looked quite differently from the ill-dressed little passenger of the "Eolus" the Monday before.

"Do look! That's the very girl we saw on the boat," went on Berenice, in the same low whisper. "Did you ever! Hasn't Mrs. Gray done her over nicely? I wonder where she got that hat?"

"I wonder what she has done with the old one?"

"Given it to the cook, or sold it to the rag-and-bottle man," retorted Berry. Then came a suppressed giggle, which ended in sudden, forced gravity as the opening words of the service fell on their ears, and they rose with the rest of the congregation.

Candace was not conscious that she was being looked at. She had only once or twice in her life been in an Episcopal church, and never before in an old one. Trinity seemed to her as wonderful and picturesque as some of the churches she had read about in books. She looked at the square pews where people sat sideways, instead of fronting the chancel as in ordinary churches. She noted the tall wands with gilded tops, which marked the places of the junior and senior wardens;

the quaint, swinging chandeliers of old brass; the tablets on the walls, two or three bearing inscriptions in honor of dead rectors or other departed worthies, one to the memory of a young girl, with a beautiful flying figure in bas-relief, carved in white marble. She gazed with amazement at the pulpit,— one of the ancient "three-decker" pattern, which is rarely seen now-a-days, with a clerk's desk below, a reading-desk above, above that a lofty pulpit for the clergyman, to which a narrow flight of stairs gave access, and suspended over all an enormous extinguisher-shaped sounding-board. It looked large and heavy enough to crush any clergyman who should be caught by its fall while in act of preaching; and Candace watched its slight oscillations with an apprehensive fascination, till she recollected that it must have hung there for a hundred years at least, so there was no reason to suppose that it would drop on this particular Sunday.

By turning her head a very little she could get a glimpse of the organ-loft, with its quaint little organ bearing two gilded mitres and a royal crown on top, and below, the inscription, "The Gift of George Berkeley, late Lord Bishop of Cloyne." She wondered who George Berkeley could have been, and resolved to ask Cousin Kate as they went home if there was any story about him.

There was no whispering or giggling in Mrs. Gray's pew. The girls were too well trained for such irreverence; and except that Georgie interchanged one little smile with Berry Joy as she came in, not one of them looked away from the clergyman till the sermon was over and the benediction pronounced. It had been an impressive service to Candace, who was used to the barer forms of the Congregational church; and she was surprised to perceive how little solemnizing effect it seemed to have on the congregation in general.

The moment people rose from their knees, a low buzz of conversation began. Berry Joy seized on Georgie and Gertrude, and began to unfold the sailing plan as they walked down the aisle. Mrs. Joy took possession of Cousin Kate. Everybody seemed to have something to say to somebody. Candace caught scraps of half-a-dozen different conversations before she reached the door, and not one of them related in any way to the sermon or to anything religious. She overheard one invitation to dinner, another to drive, an inquiry about a dressmaker, a bit of gossip about a new engagement, a request for a recipe for mayonnaise. She supposed it must be the right thing to chatter thus, since all these delightful-looking people did it; still it seemed to her country notions rather queer.

The carriage was waiting in Spring Street, a little farther up the hill. She did not like to get in till the others were ready, so she stepped aside among the gravestones, and looked up to where the white, slender spire of the old church towered against the blue. She was trying to make out the Episcopal mitre surmounted by the gilded weather-vane, when Mrs. Gray saw and beckoned to her.

She was still talking with Mrs. Joy, and that lady was saying, "I may possibly not be able to go myself, but if I am prevented I will see that the young folks have a proper matron. And then, my dear, there's Captain Davis, you know. I never let Berry sail with any one else. He's so safe and so careful, and the weather promises to be perfect."

"It certainly is perfect to-day," said Mrs. Gray. "Candace dear, I want to introduce you to Mrs. Joy. My cousin, Miss Arden, Mrs. Joy; or rather my niece, for her mother was like my own sister. She has come to spend the summer with me. Cannie, Mrs. Joy is the mother of the young lady who came down with you in the 'Eolus.'"

"Ah, indeed, the girls did not tell me about that," said Mrs. Joy. "Well, my dear,"—Mrs. Joy would have said "my dear" to Queen Victoria or the Empress of China, if she had ever had the chance of an interview with those potentates,—"you've come to a charming place and to charming relatives, I'm sure, and you can't fail to enjoy your summer. You must come with your cousins to-morrow to this sailing-party which my young folks are getting up. They'll be delighted, I'm sure."

"Thank you," said Candace, timidly, glancing at Mrs. Gray.

"That will be very nice," said her cousin. "Cannie has not been on the water yet. It is a new pleasure for her. At four o'clock, you said, Mrs. Joy?"

"Yes, dear, at four. And don't trouble to send down for the girls. It's impossible to tell exactly when they will get in, as it depends on the wind, and Berry will have the beach-wagon, and can bring them all up as well as not. Good-by, dear." And Mrs. Joy sailed toward her carriage, where the two girls were already seated.

"I've asked that Miss Arden who's staying with the Grays to go out sailing with you to-morrow," she said, as she took her seat. "You'll want another gentleman, Berry."

"Oh, mamma, what did you do that for? She's the pokiest little thing. We didn't want her at all."

"Well, Mrs. Gray introduced her, and said she was almost her niece, and I thought it seemed to be expected. Mrs. Gray is always polite to our visitors, you know, and I don't like to seem to slight any of hers. What's the matter with the girl?"

"Oh, nothing's the matter, only she's poky, and doesn't seem to fit in somehow. You would understand if you had seen her the day she came. Mrs. Gray has dressed her up, as you might be sure she would; but then she looked like the backwoods, didn't she, Ethel?"

"She seemed nice-appearing enough to-day. You'll have to make the best you can of it, I guess; for Mrs. Gray accepted for her."

"It doesn't really signify," said Berry, discontentedly; "only it throws the party all out of shape. And she's younger than any of the rest, only just seventeen, Georgie says. She'd a great deal better stay at home with Marian."

It was fortunate that Candace did not guess how unwelcome her company was to the getters-up of the party, for the idea of the sail was most delightful to her. She had never been out in a boat in her life, not even on the smallest pond; and she had just discovered the strong fascination of the sea. She longed to get nearer to it, to know it better; and in her innocent little heart she thought, "How very kind it was in Mrs. Joy to invite me."

Sunday was always a particularly pleasant day at the Grays'. Mrs. Gray was wont to declare that though she did not believe in the Jewish Sabbath, she did with all her heart believe in the Christian day of rest; and she took pains to make it a happy one for all under her roof. She gave her servants as much liberty as she could, simplified their work, and provided a plenty of good reading for such of them as stayed at home. Her own time was much more at the service of her family than it could be on ordinary days. She always took a walk with the girls in the cool of the afternoon, if the day were pleasant, and kept some book of a thoughtful kind to read aloud in the evenings. This Sunday it happened to be that wonderful little prose poem of Mrs. Oliphant's, "A Beleaguered City." Cannie found it absorbingly interesting, and even Mr. Gray laid aside his newspaper and listened to the very end.

The reading done, Candace found a chance to ask her question about George Berkeley, Bishop of Cloyne, the donor of the organ. There was a story about him, as it turned out, and a very interesting one. Mrs. Gray told how, when Dean of Derry in Ireland, the project of establishing a college in Bermuda for the education of English boys and of Indian youths to act as missionaries to their own people, had taken possession of his mind; and he had given up his preferment, and crossed the sea with his family to engage in this chosen work. She described their landing in Newport on a Sunday morning when everybody was at church, and how the clergyman stopped in the middle of his sermon, and with all his congregation following him, hurried down to the water-side to receive the distinguished guest. She promised to take Candace out some day to see Whitehall,—the house which he built on the island, and in which he lived for some years, till the impossibility of carrying out his scheme for Bermuda drove him back again to Ireland; and also the rocky shelf still called "Bishop Berkeley's Rock," where he is said to have composed the lines which begin

"Westward the course of empire takes its way."

Then she looked up a photograph from Smibert's picture of Dean Berkeley and his family to show them, and by that time the girls had all grown interested; and when Marian said that she, too, wanted to go to see Whitehall, Georgie and Gertrude begged to be included also, and Mrs. Gray promised to take them all.

"One of the Dean's little children is buried in Trinity churchyard, Cannie," she ended; "you can look up the stone some day. It has 'Lucia Berkeley' carved upon it."

"I should like to," said Cannie. "It has been so nice to hear about him. How many interesting things have happened in Newport! I shall care a great deal more about that funny little organ, next Sunday."

Newport Harbor shone all blue and silver in the sun, as the party stepped on board the cat-boat "Cornelia" at sharp four on Monday afternoon. Mrs. Fred Allen, a tall, graceful brunette, seemed as much of a girl as any of the party which she was nominally to "matronize;" but "she was married though she didn't look it," as Berry Joy remarked, and so was qualified to fill the place. There was a fair wind, which sent the boat smoothly along with little or no motion as they glided past the long sunken shoal off the end of Goat Island, and opened the view of Brenton's Cove, with the wreck of the old slaver lying in the deep shadow under one bank, opposite the ribs of the other stranded bark; while from beyond in the laughing bay, white-winged boats flitted to and fro, and seemed to beckon and make tempting signals to the poor defeated barks who might never sail or enjoy the sea again. Candace ventured to ask Gertrude in a whisper, "What are those?"

"Oh, only some old wrecks," replied Gertrude, carelessly; and she turned from Candace to talk to Tom Joy, who sat next to her.

The "Cornelia" was now running on the favoring wind between Fort Adams and the Conanicut shore. On one hand lay Newport, which looked like a dream city in the soft shine of the afternoon; on the other was the long hill line of the island, green with grasses, except where broken now and then by rocky cliffs, and indented with innumerable little coves and inlets,—some ending in strips of pebbly beach, others in stony shelves overhung by sea-weeds. The water was beautiful in color,—here pale flashing green, there purple in the shadow, with gleams of golden light and a low reach of shimmering blue toward the horizon. On sped the boat till they could almost touch the ledges. The rounded outline of the old fortification on the upper hill towered above their heads. Then suddenly she curved and wheeled off on the other tack, with the sharp line of Castle Hill and the Agassiz Point full in view.

Candace gazed with delighted eyes to left and right. Her mind was full of questions, but there seemed no one of whom she could ask them. Georgie and Berry were perched on the extreme point of the bow, with a young man stretched at their feet. Mrs. Fred was on the cabin roof amidships, with quite a little court of girls and young men about her. The couples who sat opposite and beside her seemed quite absorbed in each other. No one had spoken to Candace since the first introductions, and she was too shy to open a conversation with anybody.

"How I wish I knew!" she sighed to herself, half aloud.

Looking up, she met the shrewd, twinkling eyes of the Captain. Perhaps he had caught the words, for he asked encouragingly, "Did you speak, Miss?"

"No," said Candace, "I don't think I spoke. But I was wondering about that—that—thing up there," pointing to the Fort.

"That? That's Fort Dumpling, as folks call it. It is a kind of a queer old place, ain't it? They don't use it now for no war purposes, but it makes a pretty p'int in the landscape, and folks go there for picnics and such in the summer season."

"When was it built?" asked Candace, charmed to find somebody able and willing to satisfy her curiosity.

"Wa'al, I reckon it was about 1812, when we was a-tackling the British for the last time. 'Tain't very much of a fort to look at; but if you was to mount some of them

100

powerful guns they make now on the walls, them and the others over at Fort Adams yonder would protect the channel pretty well. The shot'd reach clear across. Why, you hardly think it perhaps, but not more'n four or five years ago, there was some folks who had come on a kind of an excursion, taking their lunches up there by Fort Dumpling, and some soldiers was firing at a long-range target over there to Fort Adams, and one of the balls came over and hit a young lady."

"How dreadful!" said Candace, her eyes measuring the long distance between the two points. "And it seems so far away. I suppose the young lady felt perfectly safe. I am sure I should have. Did it kill her?"

"Oh, no! they thought at first it had, but it didn't turn out so bad as was expected. The soldiers, they felt mighty mean, I expect. You see, they didn't intend a mite of harm to her or anybody; but it just shows how far them big guns carry now-a-days. A war-ship now, unless she was some kind of a monitor or that, would stand a fair chance of being stove and sent to the bottom before she could get in to attack Newport."

"What a fanny little house that is close down to the water!" remarked Candace, looking off to the opposite shore.

"That's Professor Agassiz's laboratory. Do y' see that kind of a cove which sets in there near by the building, and a little black thing sticking up out of it? That's the pipe of his steam-launch. He and the rest go out in it and dredge for fish and such like, and then they experiment on them inside."

"What do they do that for?" asked Candace.

"Wa'al, they want to find out about 'em, I reckon. I was in there once and saw them at work, but I couldn't make nothing out of it, and there wasn't anybody I could ask."

"Oh, what is that?" cried Candace, as the "Cornelia," tacking again, opened one of the little bays on the south end of Conanicut, where a small steam vessel was lying. Two boats, which seemed to belong to her, were rowing in a parallel line with each other, and behind them appeared a long line of bobbing points which she could not at all understand.

"That's one of the fishing steamers, and the boats are drawing her nets," explained the Captain. "Didn't you ever see a seine drawn before? Wa'al, I declare! I'm mighty glad we happened just in time, for it's a cur'us spectacle. I guess we'll kind of hang about till they get the nets in, and then I'll take the 'Cornelia' up near enough for you to see."

"Captain, there are the seine-boats out," called Tom Joy at the same moment. "Let's sail up and see what they've caught."

The two boats began to near each other as they reached the limits of the long elliptical curves which made their course; and presently a great number of scintillating specks were seen in the space enclosed between them. There were the leaping fish, just conscious that they were crowded into a confined place, and desirous of escape. When they were quite close to one another, the boats turned and began to row for the steamer. The "Cornelia" followed; and the Captain with a twist of the tiller threw her into the wind just beyond the great net, which by that time was being rapidly hauled in.

It was a wonderful thing to see,—the heavy mass of floundering fishes pouring over into the steamer's hold. Thousands and thousands of quivering silvery shapes of all kinds, from the fat, oily-bodied menhaden, to weird horned monsters with gaping mouths, and strange, half-translucent blocks like jelly, which seemed to have no mouths at all. Large and small, pinky white, black, blue,—in they poured. Now and then some fish more lucky than his fellows would splash over the side of the net and escape to liberty and the deep sea; now and then a fisherman with a sudden dash of his hand would single out a specimen choicer than the rest, a blue-fish, a chicken cod, or a sea-bass.

The little company in the sail-boat shared all the excitement of the catch. The young men left their flirtations for the boat's side, where they could get a better view. A great deal of chaff went on between Captain Davis and the captain of the menhaden steamer. Tom Joy amused himself by bargaining for blue-fish, and actually bought three big flapping specimens for a dollar and a quarter. They were deposited on the bottom of the "Cornelia," where they leaped painfully up and down, while the girls retreated for refuge to the upper deck, till Captain Davis at last caught the fish and stowed them away in his little cabin. It was not till the last loop of the seine was emptied, the last fish secured, and the boats were making ready for another cast, that the "Cornelia" finally glided away; and by that time a soft crimson glow had gathered in the west and the sun was nearing the horizon edge. The wind blew more freshly now, and with a zest and coolness which it had not had earlier in the afternoon.

Captain Davis pointed out to Candace the light-ship anchored in the offing between Point Judith and Brenton's Reef, and told her how the men who lived on board of her did not see a face from land for weeks together sometimes, when winds were stormy and waves rough. Candace listened eagerly. The rest of the party had gone back to their old places, but there was not so much chatter now. The dreamy influences of the hour were felt by every one. Dick Foster was quoting Tennyson in a low voice to pretty Julia Prime. Berry Joy and Georgie still kept up a fitful conversation with their cavalier; but Gertrude had grown silent, and Tom Joy was whistling softly to himself, with his eyes fixed on the sunset.

The "Cornelia" sped silently seaward. Suddenly they were in the shadow of a deep cove at the very end of Conanicut; and close by them rose out of the sea an immense square table of rock, over which, still as it was, the surge was constantly flinging showers of white spray. The whole top of this rock was black with large sea-birds. Candace had never imagined such a sight. The birds seemed crowding each other on every inch of space. Each moment some of them would rise, wheel in air with wild cries and screams, and then settle again to dispute for room, while the seething foam splashed over them; and the incessant flutter of their wings, the dashing spray, and the long wash of waves at the base of the rock gave to their place of refuge the effect of movement, so that it seemed to sway and float in the sea.

"Oh, what a wonderful place!" cried Candace. "Such big birds, and so many of them,—what do you call them, Captain?"

"Wa'al, they're mostly cormorants and gulls, I reckon. That's what we call them down to Newport. They ain't no good for eating, so they don't get shot; and they do increase powerfully, though it seems to me I never did see quite so many on the Kettle Bottom before as this afternoon."

"Is that the name of the rock?"

"Yes, the Kettle Bottom Rock; that's what it's called. It's a queer place. There was a painter here last summer, and he

105

made a picter of it, with them birds all flying over it, which folks said was as like as like."

The line of hotels on Narragansett Beach was now plainly in sight. They were almost off Beaver Tail, and the sea was rougher.

"Captain, we may as well put about," said Tom Joy. "The sun's going down, and there's rather more motion hereabouts than the ladies like."

So they put about and sped harborward, helped by the tide which was now running swiftly in. Frank Rivington began to sing in a mellow tenor voice little barcarolles and Venetian boat-songs, which were full of a measured rhythmic movement like oar-strokes and the beat of waves. The pink in the west deepened after the sun went down to a vivid orange red, and flamed higher and higher till the zenith caught the glow; and a little crescent moon, which was climbing up, swung like a tiny silver boat on a crimson tide. It was all like a dream, to which the noiseless speed of the boat offered no interruption.

"Good-night, Captain," said Candace, gently, as the "Cornelia" touched the wharf, at the upper end of which the carriages were waiting for them. "I'm so much obliged to you for telling me all about the things."

"You're welcome, I'm sure," replied the hearty Captain. "It's been nothing but a pleasure so far as I'm concerned. Hope I may take you out sailing again, Miss."

"Oh, I hope so. I think sailing is lovely."

"Good-by, Miss Arden. I hope you have enjoyed it," said Mrs. Allen, as she was borne off by her husband. It was the sole remark addressed by the "matron" of the party to the little stranger under her care during that afternoon; but Candace had not felt neglected.

"Oh, yes; very much, thank you," she replied. Tom Joy, who had waked up to the sense that "the little girl in the red hat" had not had much attention paid her on the sail, tried to get up a conversation as the beach-wagon climbed the hill; but Candace had but little small talk at her command, and they did not get on very fluently.

"I've had a lovely time, Miss Joy," she said shyly, as they were set down at home.

"I'm sure I'm glad. Good-night, Miss Arden." And that was all the notice which Berenice Joy took of her youngest guest, beyond the necessary good-afternoon when they first met on the wharf.

Candace was too unexacting, and too much accustomed to think of herself as a child to whom no particular attention was due, to realize or resent being treated with this scant courtesy. She told Cousin Kate about the sail and the seine steamer, and all the Captain's tales and explanations, with a glow of enjoyment which surprised Gertrude, and perhaps pricked her conscience somewhat; for that night, at hair-brushing time, she surprised Georgie by the observation, "After all, Cannie is quite a sweet little thing."

"So she is, sweet enough; but what makes you think of it just now?"

"Why, we rather left her out this afternoon, I am afraid. Hardly anybody said a word to her, except the Captain. It was rude enough of Berry, for it was her party; but I think it was worse for us. Any other girl would have been hurt and cross, and showed it; but Cannie never seemed to mind a bit, and enjoyed everything, and was just as nice and pleasant as if she had been the belle of the party."

"Well, it was too bad," said Georgie, penitently. "I never thought about it, and I sat ever so far off from her, and Arnold Foster was so funny—in fact, I forgot Cannie. I took it for granted that she was being entertained, somehow."

"I'm afraid both of us find it pretty easy to forget Cannie," remarked Gertrude. "Well, I shall try to do better another time."

CHAPTER VI.
A TALK ABOUT SHYNESS.

CANNIE," said Mrs. Gray, a few days after the sailing-party, "would you like to study French this summer, with Marian for company?"

"Y-es," replied Cannie; but she said it more because she saw that a yes was expected of her, than because of any real pleasure at the idea. Like most girls who have had scanty or poor teaching, she liked to read a great deal better than she liked to study.

"Do you know any French at all?" continued her cousin.

"No, not any. There wasn't anybody at home who taught it; and if there had been, I don't believe Aunt Myra would have let me learn. She thinks English is a good enough language for anybody. I did study Latin a little while, though. Aunt Myra consented to that, because we had papa's Latin books in the house, and she said they might as well be useful."

"Well, your Latin won't come amiss to your French," said Mrs. Gray, laughing to herself over this thrifty reason for learning a language. "Marian is, of course, far ahead of you in speaking, for she learned it by ear, as they say of music, during the year we spent in France on our way home; but she knows but little of the rules and grammar. I think you will do very well together; for her fluency will tempt you on to talk, and your perseverance will keep her up to the exercises and conjugations, which are sad drudgery, but very needful if you are ever really to know anything of the language. You are persevering, are you not, Cannie?"

"I don't know whether I am or not," replied Candace, inly resolving to justify Cousin Kate's good opinion.

"I have confidence in you," said Mrs. Gray, smiling kindly at her. "And another thing I wanted to say is, that I think both you and Marian will enjoy the summer a great deal better for having one regular study to prepare for. It gives a sort of backbone to your lives, don't you see? Clear fun is like clear honey,—it cloys and loses its charm; but when it is mixed with occupation it keeps its flavor, and you don't get tired of it."

"I can understand that," said Candace, thoughtfully. "I recollect how nice Saturday afternoons used to seem when Aunt Myra had kept me busy darning stockings all the morning. I think I would like the French lessons, Cousin Kate; only I am afraid the teacher will think me very stupid."

Candace's fears were not realized. As a beginner, her first steps were necessarily slow; but she took pains, and had no bad habits or evil accents to unlearn, and after a while she "got hold" of the language and went on more rapidly. Marian's fluent chatter stimulated her to try to talk as fast also, though Mademoiselle Bougereau, their teacher, found a great deal of fault with Marian, and said that many of the phrases which came so glibly out of her mouth partook of the nature of slang, and were not finished or elegant French. Still, with all drawbacks, the little class of two made fair progress; and Candace realized that what Mrs. Gray had said was true, and that all the bits of amusement and pleasure which came in her way were doubly enjoyed by reason of the little "backbone" of real work thus put into her days.

Another pleasure which she and Marian shared in common was a surf-bath before breakfast. Berry Joy had got up an omnibus party of girls, which she called "The Early Dip Club," in which all four of Mrs. Gray's young people were included. Punctually at a quarter before seven on every fair morning the omnibus rattled up the Avenue; and the "Club" set out, under the care of an old experienced maid of Mrs. Joy's, who had nursed Berry, and could be trusted to see that none of the young ladies did anything very imprudent,— such as staying too long in the water or standing about in their wet bathing-dresses. At that early hour there were no loungers to stare at the party. The beach, cleanly swept by the tide of the night before, had scarcely a footprint to mar its smooth, firm sands. There was something delightful in the perfect freshness of the hour and place. Some of the girls had taken lessons in the "School of Natation" in the lower bay, and could swim very well. Candace could not swim, and made no attempt to learn; but she soon acquired the art of floating, under the tuition of Alice Frewen, who, next to Marian and herself, was the youngest of the party, and to whom she had taken a great fancy. The three "children," as Berenice Joy called them, made common cause, and generally kept together, a little apart from the others, holding each other's hands and splashing up and down in the rollers with great enjoyment.

Bathing over, the "Early Dippers" returned home in their omnibus about the time that other people were waking up, bringing with them such cheeks and such appetites as were a satisfaction to their families, and did great credit to the powers of the Newport surf.

So the days sped on. It was full summer-tide now; yet the weather never seemed hot, except perhaps for an hour or two at a time. Morning after morning the sun would rise in a blaze of yellow, which anywhere else would have betokened a scorching day; and just as people had begun to say, "What a sultry morning!" lo, in one moment the wind would set in from the sea, strong, salty, fresh, invigorating; and, behold, it was cool! Or if the afternoon seemed for a little while oppressive in the streets of the old town, it was only necessary to go down to the end of the Avenue to find a temperature cool enough to be called chilly. Nobody ever thought of driving without a shawl, and the shawl was almost always needed. Mrs. Gray was wont to say that Newport had three different climates,—a warm one and a cold one and an in-between one,—and it had them all three every day, and people could take their choice, which was much more convenient than having only one.

The large places on the Cliffs were all open and occupied now. The flower-beds, newly planted when Candace came, made wonderful spaces of color everywhere in the emerald turf. Geraniums seemed as universal as grass, and their splendid reds and pinks were such as are seldom seen anywhere except in Newport. Foliage plants grew into enormous crimson or golden mats, which showed not one break in their luxuriant fulness. In the more ornate places were beds planted to look like Turkish carpets or Indian shawls, the pattern reproduced by hundreds of small plants of carefully adjusted hues, kept closely shaven so as to lie as flat as the objects they simulated. Roses were everywhere; and the soft drifting mists which now and again blew in from the sea, and the constant underlying moisture of the climate kept everything in a state of perfect freshness.

The Casino balls and lawn-tennis matches had begun. Visitors were pouring into the Ocean House; and every day increased the number of carriages, drags, dog-carts, pony phaetons, and village carts, which on all bright afternoons thronged the Avenue from end to end. Dinners and lawn-parties were of frequent occurrence, and during calling-hours the bell seemed always in vibration at the Gray cottage.—

"Cottage" I call it; for in Newport everything that is not a "villa" is styled a "cottage," no matter how big or square or uncompromising its appearance may be.

Candace was rather too young to be taken into general society, and she saw much less of these entertainments than Georgie; less even than Gertrude, who, by reason of her intimacy with Georgie's set, was often included in their parties, though not yet formally "out." Mrs. Gray, however, thought it good for Candace to share a little of what was going on; and she took pains to have her invited now and then with the others to lawn-parties, excursions, or afternoon teas. If Mrs. Gray herself was present on these occasions, Cannie did pretty well; for she invariably got behind her cousin or beside her, made no attempt to talk, and just amused herself by watching what went on. But when Mrs. Gray did not go, and she was left to the tender mercies of Georgie and Gertrude, she was apt to feel lonely and unfriended; for with all the better resolutions of these pleasure-loving young people, they still found it "easy to forget Cannie."

"What are you going to do this morning, children?" asked Mrs. Gray, one day at breakfast. "Is the great tennis-match that we have heard so much about to come off, or have I forgotten the date?"

"No, this is the eventful day," replied Gertrude; "and I am so nervous about it that I don't feel as if I could play at all."

"Nonsense! you played beautifully yesterday," said Georgie.

"There wasn't anything depending on me yesterday. It is queer how people never do their best when it is important that they should. I feel as if I were going to be all thumbs this morning."

"Oh, you won't. You'll get excited and forget about the thumbs," remarked Georgie, consolingly. "Mamma, aren't you coming to see us?"

"Yes, I think I shall; and I will bring Cannie with me. She hasn't seen the Casino yet."

Candace had become familiar with the street side of the pretty Casino building, and admired greatly its long façade, with the quaintly shingled curves and balconies, and the low gables, ornamented with disks and half suns in dull gilding,—all looking, Mrs. Gray said, as old as if it had stood there for a couple of centuries, instead of for three or four years only. But the street side, picturesque as it is, had by no means prepared her for what she saw as she followed her cousin through the entrance hall and into the quadrangle beyond.

What did she see? An open space of greenest turf, broken only by two long curving beds of foliage plants and a stone basin from which a fountain threw up a cool jet to refresh the air. On either hand, and on the side from which they had entered, was a line of low buildings, with balconies and grilles of quaintly designed wood-work, windows filled with oddly tinted glass, and at one point a clock tower of rough masonry, over which vines were clustering. Connecting the buildings to right and left, was a raised covered gallery, semi-circular in shape, with a second gallery overhead; and on these ladies in fresh morning toilettes were sitting, some with pieces of embroidery in their hands, others collected in knots for conversation or to listen to the music of the band.

Beyond this gallery lay another and much larger quadrangle, with lines of trees and shrubs to veil its boundaries, on which lawn-tennis was being played in five or six courts at once. At the back of this quadrangle was another long low building, in the same picturesque style as the rest, which, Mrs. Gray explained, contained on one side a charming little theatre which could also be used as a ball-room, and on the other an admirable bowling-alley and racket-court for the use of the members. The band was playing gay music; a hum of conversation filled the air; pretty girls in white or blue or rose color were moving about; the wind drew with delicious coolness through the galleries; altogether it would have been hard to find on a summer morning a prettier place or a livelier scene.

Mrs. Gray was too much of a favorite not to be at once sought out. She was soon the centre of a little group of friends; and Candace sat beside her, silent as usual, but gazing with enchanted eyes at the animated figures on the tennis ground, at the gables and loggias of the restaurant building, at the curious clock-tower, with the heavy iron rings depending above the base, and its top like a bellflower. It was all like a fairy tale to her. Her imagination was actively at work, but no one would have guessed it from her quiet little face; and when Mrs. Gray introduced her to one person and another, she shrank into herself, and after her shy little bow and "How do you do?" relapsed again into stillness, and made no attempt to keep up a conversation. People were kind; but it is always easy to secure solitude in a crowd, and Cannie soon found herself let alone to her heart's content.

Gertrude was playing her best. Her nervousness had disappeared in the excitement of the game, as Georgie had predicted that it would, and some of her strokes were so clever as to win a little volley of applause from the by-standers. Candace did not know the game well enough to appreciate fine points of play, but she could perfectly appreciate the fun of winning; and when Gertrude, flushed and radiant, came to show her mother the prize she had won, a lace pin of gold filigree in the form of a racket, Cannie's face lighted up with a bright sympathy which was pleasant to see. A lady who had been watching her whispered to Mrs. Gray, "What a sweet face that little niece of yours has!"

"So she has," replied Mrs. Gray; "only she is so very timid. She never does herself justice."

"Is it timidity? I had a fancy that she had an unhappy temper, or was troubled about something. Her face has always seemed so sad and overcast till just now, when it lit up at Gertrude's good fortune, and then I caught the true expression."

Mrs. Gray recollected this remark as she drove home with Candace, who, perfectly at ease now that she was alone with her cousin Kate, chattered and laughed like any other girl, and showed herself the happy young thing that she was. At home, even when with Georgie and Gertrude, she was no longer shy; but the moment a stranger came in, all was changed. It was like an evil spell cast by some enchanter. The pleasant smile and simple childish manner vanished, and Cannie became stiff, cold, awkward even; for her discomfort made her feel constrained in every limb and muscle. Her manner grew frigid, because she was frightened and wanted to hide it. If she had to shake hands, she did it without smiling and with downcast eyes; she was too ill at ease to be cordial. People thought that she was out of humor or troubled about something, and set her down as dull and unattractive; and with a natural reaction, Cannie felt that they did not like her, and that made her more uncomfortable than ever.

Mrs. Gray pitied Cannie very much, and had tried various methods to shake her out of her shyness and teach her confidence in herself. None of them so far had done any good. She now began to wonder if her analysis of the case was not wrong; if shyness was not a fault rather than a misfortune, and needed to be disciplined accordingly. She watched Candace for a day or two, and then she made up her mind. "It will be kill or cure," she thought, as she ordered the coupé and proposed to Cannie to take the ocean drive. Marian wanted to go too, and protested that there was plenty of room on the little let-down seat, and that she wouldn't crowd them a bit; but her mother was quite firm, and despatched her on an errand in the other direction without any compunctions.

"I must have Cannie all to myself," she thought.

It was not till they were out of the Avenue and rolling along the smooth road beyond Bailey's Beach, with the fresh-water ponds on one hand and on the other the points and indentations of the coast, that Mrs. Gray led to the subject which was on her mind. The sea was intensely blue that afternoon, with shoots of creamy foam over every rock and ledge, and for a while they talked of nothing but the beauty of the day and the view. Finally Mrs. Gray began,—

"How did you like Mrs. Endicott?"

Mrs. Endicott was one of various visitors who had called that morning. Candace had been sent for, and had been more than usually awkward and unresponsive.

"I liked her pretty well," said Candace. "She didn't talk to me but a little while."

"I know she didn't. It was on her account specially that I sent for you to come down," continued Mrs. Gray. "Did she tell you that she was at school with your mother when they were quite little girls?"

"No!" said Candace, surprised.

"Yes; they were great friends, and she wrote to me before she came up that she was looking forward to seeing you. Shall I tell you why she so soon stopped talking to you? She told me afterward. She said: 'I wanted to talk to your niece about her mother, and to ask her to come to me for a visit; but she looked so frightened and seemed so stiff and shy and hard to get at, that I thought the kindest thing I could do would be to let her alone for the moment, till she was a little more used to me, and to talk to some one else. Next time I come, we shall get on better, I hope.'"

Candace looked much mortified.

"Was I stiff?" she asked. "I didn't know it. I didn't mean to be."

"You are almost always stiff with strangers," said her cousin. "I know you do not mean it, and you are not conscious of the effect of your own manner; but all the same it is stiff. Now, Cannie, will you promise me not to be hurt at what I am going to say?"

"Why, of course I won't," said Cannie, looking at her with trustful eyes.

"Well then, listen! If I didn't know you,—if you were not my own dear little Cannie, whose warm heart I am sure of, and whose good intentions I know all about,—if I met you for the first time and judged of you merely from your manner, as all strangers must judge,—do you know what I should think?"

"What?"

"I should think you rather a cold-hearted girl, who didn't like people and didn't mind letting them know it."

"Oh, Cousin Kate!"

"Or else, if I were more charitably inclined, I should think you a dull girl who did not take much interest in what went on about her."

"Oh, Cousin Kate!"

"Or," continued her cousin, relentlessly, "if I were a real angel, and disposed to make the very best of everybody, I should say to myself, 'The poor thing is so shy that she can't show what she really is.' Unluckily, there are few perfect angels in this world, and a great many of the other sort. And even as a perfect angel, my dear Cannie, I don't think I should consider you exactly agreeable."

"But what can I do?" demanded Candace, looking very unhappy. "I can't make myself not shy."

"No; but you can mend matters by forcing yourself to hide your shyness. I have been meditating on the subject,

Cannie, and I have made up my mind that shyness is one form of selfishness."

"Cousin Kate, how can you say that? I thought selfishness was doing what you liked and what is pleasant. I'm sure I don't like to be shy."

"Oh, it's not that kind of selfishness," said Mrs. Gray, smiling. "There is nothing pleasant about shyness; that I am quite ready to admit. But can't you see that it is self-occupation, the being absorbed with your own sensations and feelings, and with trying to imagine what people are thinking about you, that makes you so miserable? If you could forget and occupy yourself with others, this shyness would go. Now, this morning, had you been full of Mrs. Endicott, and what she was like, and what she wanted to talk about, instead of little Candace Arden, and what Mrs. Endicott considered her like, it would all have been different, and much pleasanter for both of you."

"Oh, if I only could," said Candace, with a catch in her voice, "I would give anything I have in the world! I hate to seem so awkward and dull. But you've no idea how uncomfortable I feel, Cousin Kate. The moment I come downstairs and see that roomful of company, my face twitches and my cheeks burn, and I can't think of anything to say, and I keep wishing I could run upstairs again and hide somewhere."

"Yes, because, as I said, your mind is full of yourself. If instead of coming in with this miserable self-consciousness full upon you, you could look upon the roomful as just so many people to whom you owe the little duties of politeness and cordiality, for whom you have the chance to do something kind or pleasant, you would forget your face and your cheeks and the desire to run away. You would be thinking of them, and in thinking of them you would forget to be shy."

Candace did not reply.

"You are a conscientious child," her cousin went on. "I think that you sincerely wish to do what is right, and to make God's rule the rule of your life. And, Candace, in my opinion you should consider it a part of religious duty to try to get rid of this false shame, this bondage to the idea of self, and to learn to live for others instead."

Candace looked up, with the dawn of a new idea in her face.

"How do you mean?" she asked.

"You cannot always run away," continued her cousin. "Big as it is, the world is not big enough to furnish hiding-places for all the people who are afraid to face their fellow-men. And since you cannot run away, your plain duty is to be brave and make the best of it. Now, Cannie, there are two things which may help you to do this, two thoughts which you can keep in mind; and I wish you would try to remember them when you feel a fit of fright or of stiffness coming on."

"What are they?"

"One is, that you are but one little insignificant atom among thousands. People are not thinking about you or noticing you very particularly. You are not of much consequence except to yourself and the few friends who love you. This would be a mortifying fact, if vanity were your trouble; but as it is not, it is a comfortable one. And just as nobody notices you specially, so all the world is not engaged afterward in recollecting all your little mistakes and the stupid things you have said. Unless you have done something very queer, they forget about you as soon as they lose sight of you. I know what miseries sensitive girls undergo in thinking over their foolish speeches and actions, and imagining that every one remembers them as distinctly as they themselves do."

Cannie couldn't help smiling. "Cousin Kate, how can you know about all those things?" she asked.

"Because I was a girl myself once, and as foolish as any of the rest of you; and I have not forgotten how it feels to be a girl," said her cousin, gayly. "That is the use of growing old, Cannie. You can show the way to younger people, and make the road you have walked over a little easier for them.—But to go back to what we were talking about, our own insignificance is one helpful thought, as I said; the other is, that kindliness is one of the Christian virtues, and it is just as much a duty to practise it as it is to be honest and temperate."

Candace drew a long breath.

"It would be perfectly delightful to keep thinking like that always," she said; "the only thing is that I am afraid I should forget when the time came. I wish you could give me an exact rule, Cousin Kate, just what to say and how to act. I would try ever so hard to follow it."

"I know you would," said Mrs. Gray; "but there is no exact rule that I can give, except the Golden one, to do to others just as you would like them to do to you. If you feel stiff, be sure to look cordial. Smile, and shake hands as if you meant it. Try to look interested in what people are saying to you. A good listener helps on conversation as well as a good talker. If you are friendly and warm in your manner, other people will warm to you instinctively. Try it, Cannie, and see if I am not right. And now we will not talk any more about ourselves or our shyness, but drive into the Fort and listen to the music. I caught a strain from the Band just then, and I recollect that this is a 'Fort Day.'"

So in they drove, clattered between walls and embankments, and over a steep paved incline beneath a great arch, and found themselves in an open square, with buildings of solid masonry on all sides, in the midst of which the band was stationed. Other carriages were drawn up to listen to the music, and officers in uniform were coming and going, and talking to the ladies in the carriages. One of these officers, a nice old Major, with a bald spot under his gold-banded cap, knew Mrs. Gray, and came to welcome her. His "girls" were gone over to Newport to a lawn-party, he said; but he insisted on taking Mrs. Gray and Cannie in to see their quarters, which were in a casemate, in close neighborhood to one of the great guns. Here he brewed them a delicious cup of tea; and afterward, at Mrs. Gray's request, he took Candace to see the magazines, and some of the curious underground passages which connect one side of the Fort with the other. Cannie thought these extremely interesting, and like all the caves on desert islands which she had ever read about; for they were narrow, dark, and mysterious, they smelt very close, and all sorts of odd funguses and formations were growing on the roofs overhead.

These adventures chased the worry from her mind and the anxious puckers from her forehead; and she went home quite happily, without recurring again to the subject of their late conversation. But she did not forget it, and it bore fruit. Mrs. Gray noted, without seeming to be on the watch, the efforts which Candace thenceforward made to overcome her shyness. She saw her force herself to come forward, force herself to smile, to speak, when all the time she was quaking inwardly; and she felt that there was real power of character required for such an effort. Quiet Candace would always be;

modest and retiring it was her nature to be: but gradually she learned not to seem cold and stiff; and when her cousin saw her, as she sometimes did, forgetting herself in talking to some one, and lighting up into her easy, natural, bright manner, she felt that the rather hard lesson administered that afternoon on the ocean drive had not been in vain. Rome was not built in a day, and ease of manner is not acquired in a moment; but Candace had at last got hold of a right idea, and there was hope that with time people less charitable even than "perfect angels" might pronounce her "agreeable."

CHAPTER VII.
TWO PICNICS.

IT was while Candace was still doing battle with her shyness, sometimes getting the better of it and then again yielding and letting it get the better of her, that Georgie and Gertrude sent out invitations to another luncheon party of girls. It was the third they had given since coming to Newport. Mrs. Gray certainly did a great deal for the pleasure of her daughters, although Berenice Joy did consider her so "strict."

Candace had her share in this entertainment, as one of the three young ladies of the house. The party was mainly composed of the "Early Dippers," who were not as formidable to her imagination as entire strangers would have been. She and Georgie and Gertrude wore their white woollen dresses, which were almost exactly alike, and "looked like triplets," as Marian rather spitefully observed. Marian herself was not asked to the party, and was out of humor in consequence. Her crossness did not extend to Candace, however. She evinced this by coming in just as Candace had finished dressing, with a long-stemmed pink rose in her hand, which she pinned on the shoulder of the white gown, just under Candace's cheek.

"That looks sweet," remarked Marian. "I am really quite pleased at your appearance; you're every bit as pretty as Gertrude, and heaps better looking than that old Georgie, who wouldn't let me come to her party. Now, take my advice: hold your head up, and don't let any of the girls bully you. If Berry Joy tries it, sit down hard on her."

"I don't know how to sit down hard," laughed Candace; but she kissed Marian for the sweet rose, and went downstairs feeling quite brave. Marian watched her over the balusters; made a face at Berry Joy, who was just sailing into the drawing-room; shook her dimpled fist at Georgie's back, visible through the open door; and then went to sit with her mother, who also was "not invited."

There is no prettier entertainment than a lunch-party of girls. The flowers, the confections, all the graceful little fripperies of the feast, seem to suit with the bright young faces, to whom daylight is a becoming and not a dangerous test. Frederic had taken great pains in ornamenting the table for his young ladies. There was a nosegay for each guest, and no two nosegays were alike. One was made up of roses and daisies, another of roses and heliotrope, another of roses and violets; and each was tied with a satin ribbon of corresponding color, which had the name of the girl for whom it was intended, and the date, painted in gold letters on the ends. In the middle of the table stood a large square pan of glass, in which floated a mass of waterlilies, pink and white; and winding in and out among the little dishes of crystallized fruits, éclairs, apricots, and hot-house grapes, was a continuous curving wreath of pansies of every color. It appeared to lie directly on the white tablecloth; but the stems of the flowers were really set in shallow semi-circles of tin, not over half an inch high, which were filled with wet sand.

For the more substantial part of the meal appeared a succession of appetizing little dishes, hot and perfectly served; and the wind-up of the whole was, of course, unlimited ice-cream and water-ices, those national delicacies dear equally to the heart of every American girl the country over, whether she consumes her saucer-full in uppermost Maine or southernmost Florida.

Luncheon over, the party went out to the piazza, where coffee was served; and then Berry Joy began to tell of a picnic at Southwick's grove which she had attended the day before. None of the other girls had, as it happened, been present; so she had the field of narrative to herself.

"It was perfectly splendid," she said. "There were five coaches with four ladies and a lot of men in each, and ever so many other carriages. We made a sort of procession down the Island. I went in Lawrence Jones's coach, with Sue Tucker and Maude and Mrs. Freddy. You should have seen the country people rush out to look at us when all the horns blew at once. I tell you it was exciting."

"And what did you do after you got to the grove?"

"Oh, we had the most wonderful spread that ever was seen. You know, everybody takes a dish and a bottle of wine to these picnics; and there is always a great competition as to who shall bring the best things. I never saw such a luncheon in my life; everything was perfectly delicious."

"But what did you do?"

"Do? Why, we didn't do anything but that. There was no time for anything else. It took ever so long to get lunch ready. Some of the things had to be cooked after we got there, you know, and the coffee and the mayonnaise made. The servants lit fires and fussed about, and the rest of us sat round and talked a little; but I was so ravenous that I couldn't think of anything but lunch, and I rather think the others were in the same condition. Then, as soon as we had done, it was time to start for home."

"What do you think that horrid Mr. Deane said?" she continued, after a short pause. "You know, he's always trying to be satirical. Some one was saying something about the grove's being such a nice place for picnics, and Mr. Deane interrupted, in that disagreeable dry way of his which some people call funny: 'Well, yes, perhaps so; but in my opinion the proper place for a picnic of this kind is—a gorge!'"

There was a universal giggle.

"How did he dare?" observed Julia Prime.

"Oh, he dares to say just what he likes. He doesn't mind anybody. But I know one thing, and that is that Gorham Allerton didn't like it a bit. He looked absolutely black, and I saw him talking to Mrs. Jackson Tainter about it afterward; and I'll wager something handsome that old Deane will find himself left out of the next picnic. I'm sure, if he does, it will only serve him right for being so rude."

"I don't believe he'll mind it if he isn't invited," remarked Gertrude. "He dined with papa last night; and I heard him say that it was the dullest affair he ever was at in his life, and only fit for the 'companions of Ulysses.'"

"What did he mean?"

"I don't know. Something about General Grant, I suppose.—Candace, what are you laughing at?"

"Oh, nothing," said Cannie, composing her face as well as she could. A little old translation of the Odyssey had been among the books in the North Tolland library, and she was more "up" in the "companions of Ulysses" than the rest of the party.

"How different picnics now-a-days are from those which we used to have in Newport when I was a girl," remarked Mrs. Gray from the drawing-room window, where she had been standing unperceived for a moment or two.

"Oh, Mrs. Gray, are you there?" and the girls hastened to the window. Some of them kissed her; and all, except perhaps Berry Joy, looked glad to see her, for she was a general favorite with her daughters' friends.

"Tell us about the picnics you used to have when you were young," said Julia Prime, balancing herself on the window-sill and keeping fast hold of Mrs. Gray's hand.

"There is not much to tell, Julia. They would seem tame affairs enough to you modern young people, I suppose. We hadn't any men with us as a general thing, except an occasional brother or cousin, and we didn't carry half as much to eat as seems to be considered necessary now-a-days. Then we did all the work ourselves instead of taking cooks and footmen to do it for us; but for all that, we thought them most delightful. For one thing, we always went to some really interesting place, such as the Glen, or the Dumpling Rocks, or the Paradise Valleys."

"Where are the Paradise Valleys?" inquired Julia.

"Oh, I know what they are," said Maud Hallett. "They are lovely places hidden in behind Bishop Berkeley's Rock. I went there once with Aunt Edith. She knows all the nooks and corners of Newport better than anybody else."

"Mamma, you must take us there some day," said Georgie.

"Oh, do, and let me go with you," pleaded Maud. "I should like so much to see them again."

"Won't you take me too?" said Belle Jeffrys.

"We should all like to go," remarked Julia, slyly. "Oh, Mrs. Gray, dear, I have such a lovely idea! Give us a picnic yourself, one of the nice old-fashioned sort that you used to have when you were young, in the Paradise Valley; won't you, dear Mrs. Gray? Oh, do!"

"You needn't coax so hard, Julia; I'm very easy to persuade when I like to do a thing," said Mrs. Gray, with a laugh. "I'll give you a picnic with pleasure; only I must make one stipulation, that it shall be exclusively a girl-party. I don't think the young men of the present day would enjoy the kind of thing I mean, or know what to make of it."

"Girls!" cried Julia, "just listen to what this dear angel says! She's going to take us to Paradise Valley, all by ourselves, with no men to bother and distract our attention.—Men are out of place in Paradise anyway; just think how Adam behaved! (this in a parenthesis).—It is to be a real old-fashioned "goloptious" picnic. Now, who would like to go besides myself?"

"I, I, I," cried the girls, with gratifying unanimity.

"Now, what day shall it be?" continued Julia. "Let's make Mrs. Gray settle the time at once, and then she can't back out."

"I don't want to back out," said Mrs. Gray. "I enjoy the idea as much as you do."

So, after some comparing of engagements, the next Thursday was fixed upon.

"You had better make this the rendezvous," said the giver of the picnic. "I shall have room for one girl in my wagonette besides my four. You must all wear something stout, which won't spoil with scrambling over rocks, and you need not bring any luncheon-baskets. I will see to all that. This is to be an old-fashioned picnic, you know, and I shall provide exactly the sort of things that we used to take

'When I was young and charming, many years ago.'"

"You are just as charming as you can be now," declared Belle, enthusiastically.

"I do hope there won't be a fog," said Julia Prime, as she walked up the Avenue with the others.

"I sha'n't care if there is," replied Berry. "I must say it sounds to me like a very stupid plan,—no men, and nothing in particular to eat. It's just like Mrs. Gray. Her ideas are so queer, as mamma says."

"I wonder you go if you feel that way about it," retorted Julia.

"I dare say I sha'n't. I have a strong presentiment that on that particular day I shall have a headache."

And Berry did,—a "distracting" headache, as she wrote Georgie over-night. She was the only member of the Early Dip Club who missed the picnic. Headaches are sad but convenient things.

Eleven o'clock brought the girls to the Grays' front door, all ready for their start, in various village carts and victorias. There was a little re-distribution: Georgie and Gertrude fitted in with some of their cronies, and Mrs. Gray took three girls besides Marian and Candace in her wagonette. Frederic and the coachman stowed many small baskets and a heap of wraps into the different rumbles and box seats, and they set forth under the bluest of blue skies. It was a beautiful day, just warm enough and not too warm; for a fragrant wind was blowing softly in from the sea.

They had passed the first beach, which at that hour was black with bathers and by-standers, and had climbed the hill-slope which separates it from the second beach, when Marian suddenly cried, "Mamma, here we are close to Purgatory; can't we stop just a minute and show it to Candace?"

Mrs. Gray looked at her watch.

"Your minute will be at least a quarter of an hour, Marian," she said; "but I think there is time enough. Would any of the rest of you like to go?"

Girls always "want to go." There was a general disembarkation; and Mrs. Gray led the way through a gate and across a rough field which stretched along the top of a line of cliffs, steeper and bolder than those on the Newport Point, and cut here and there into sudden sharp fissures.

The scanty grass, yellow with August sun, was broken everywhere by lumps and boulders of that odd conglomerate which is known by the name of "plum-pudding stone." Golden-rod and the early blue aster were flowering everywhere. A flock of sheep fled at their approach, with a low rushing sound like the wind in boughs.

Purgatory.
The name of "Purgatory" seemed to her to suggest some terrible
sort of place.

Candace walked along with the rest, in a little shiver of expectancy. The name of "Purgatory" seemed to her to suggest some terrible sort of place. Presently she saw the girls ahead, as they reached a particular point, diverge sharply to the right with little cries and exclamations; and when she advanced, she found herself on the edge of a chasm deeper and darker than any of those which they had passed. It cut the cliff from its highest point to the sea-level; and the wall-like sides receded toward their base, leaving vaulted hollows beneath, into which the eye could not penetrate. Only the ear caught the sound of thunderous murmurs and strange gurgles and hisses of spray echoing from unseen recesses far underground; and it was easy to imagine that these sounds came from some imprisoned sea-creature, hemmed in by the tide, with no chance of escape, and vexing the air with its groans.

Candace shrank away from the brink with a sensation of affright. "What an awful place!" she said, drawing a long breath. "Do you suppose any one ever fell down there?"

Every member of the party had some tradition of the sort to relate; but none of the stories seemed to rest on a very secure foundation.

"Anybody who did must be killed, I should think. I don't wonder they named it Purgatory," said Marian.

There was a fascination of horror about the spot. The girls lingered and leaned over the brink and turned back, until Mrs. Gray had to call them away; and they were all rather silent as they walked across the field to their carriages. But the impression was soon dispelled; for as they drove down the incline toward the second beach, they came upon an unexpected scene of brilliant and animated life.

The tide and the wind together were bringing ashore quantities of seaweed of the kind used in manuring fields, and all the farmers of the neighborhood had assembled to secure this heaven-planted harvest. The long curves of yellow sands which stretch from the Purgatory rocks to Sacluest Point were alive with people. Teams of mild mouse-colored or white oxen stood harnessed to heavy wagons, ready to drag the seaweed home. Out in the plunging surf men were urging horses seaward, or swimming them toward the shore, with long rake-like implements in their wake, which gathered and bore along masses of the glittering brown and rosy kelp. The splash and foam of the waves, the rearing horses, the cries of the men and of the seagulls, who seemed to resent this intrusion upon their haunts, made a vivid and fascinating picture, which seemed in keeping with the beauty of sea and sky and the freshness of the sun-warmed wind.

Then, passing the beach, the carriages drove along a smooth country road for a short distance, and turned into a narrow lane running up hill, which presently brought them to a small farm-house built on the very edge of a ravine.

"Here we take to our feet," said Mrs. Gray, jumping out of the wagonette.

The farmer and his wife, who seemed to be old acquaintances, came out to speak to her. The baskets were collected, and the carriages sent back to town, with orders to return to the same place at six o'clock.

"Oh, why six? why not stay and go home by moonlight?" urged Julia.

"My dear child, if you were in the habit of reading either the almanac or the heavens, you would know that there will be no moon to-night till after eleven o'clock," said her chaperone. "These roads will be as black as pitch by half-past seven. Now, girls, each of you take your own shawl and one of the baskets, and we will descend into Paradise. It sounds paradoxical, but you shall see."

She led the way down a steep narrow pathway on the hill-side into the valley below. The path was overhung with trees. It was necessary to put the boughs aside here and there; brambles reached from the thicket to catch at the girls' skirts as they went by; but when they had passed these trifling obstacles they found themselves safely on the level floor of a little valley below.

Such a choice little valley! It was enclosed between the line of hill from which they had just descended and another parallel line, whose top was of solid granite and whose base was walled by trees. This double barrier kept off all cold winds, and let the sunshine in from east to west to flood and foster the valley growths. To the east the eye saw only the winding of the leafy glade; the west stood open to the sea, and gave a wide vista of glittering ocean and yellow surf-fringed beach.

The ground was carpeted with the softest grass. Thickets of wild roses showed here and there a late blossom, and other thickets of alders glittered with coral-red berries. Apple-trees loaded with small crimson apples made spots of color on the hill-side. Wild-flowers grew thickly in damp spots, and mosses clustered among the stones. Birds chirped and flew from every bush and tree. All was shaded and peaceful and still. Newport, with its whirl and glitter, seemed immeasurably far away. The Paradise Valley might to all appearance have been hidden in the heart of the Alleghanies, instead of being within three miles of the gayest watering-place in America!

Mrs. Gray, with accustomed feet, led the way straight across the glade to where an old cedar-tree stood commanding the oceanward view, with a square block of stone at its foot.

"This is where we used always to come," she said, in a dreamy voice.

"What a delicious place!" cried Julia; "to think that I should have spent seven summers in Newport and never have seen it before! What shall we do with the baskets, Mrs. Gray, dear?"

"Put them here in the shade, and when you all feel hungry we will open them."

"Hungry! why, I am as hungry as a wolf at this moment. I have a gift at being ravenous. Girls, what do you say? Don't you agree with me that no time is like the present time for lunch? Hold up your hands if you do."

"Very well," said Mrs. Gray, laughing, as every hand flew up. "We will have lunch at once, then; but I warn you that there is a good deal to be done first. There," pointing to a blackened spot against a rock, "is where we always boiled our kettle. If some of you will collect some dry sticks, we will see if the present generation is capable of making a fire. I meanwhile will fetch the water."

She took a bright little copper kettle from one of the baskets, and mounted the hill with elastic footsteps, calling out, as she went,—

"Make haste, and be sure that the sticks are dry."

"I'm not sure that I know a dry stick when I see it," whispered Maud Hallett to Julia; but instinct, as often happens, took the place of experience on this occasion, and Mrs. Gray found quite a respectable pile of fuel awaiting her when she came back with her kettle full of spring water.

"Now I will show you how to swing a pot over the fire," she said; and in three minutes a rustic crane of boughs was constructed, the kettle was hanging from it, and the wood piled artistically underneath. A box of matches appeared from Mrs. Gray's pocket, which; as Marian said, was every bit as good as the "Bag" of the Mother in the "Swiss Family Robinson," and seemed to hold almost as great a variety of useful things. Presently a gay little fire was crackling and snapping against the face of the rock, and adding its smoke to the blackened stains left by those other smokes of long ago. The girls stood about, watching the blaze and listening for the first hiss of the kettle; but Mrs. Gray informed them that there was still work to be done.

"I want some new potatoes to roast, for one thing," she said. "Maud and Georgie, you might run up to the farm and ask Mr. Bacon to send me a few, say eighteen or twenty large ones,—oh, and a couple of dozen fresh eggs."

While they were absent on this errand, the other girls, under Mrs. Gray's direction, unpacked the baskets and arranged their contents on the rock beneath the cedar-tree. Mrs. Gray had taken pains to provide, as far as was possible, the same sort of food which twenty-odd years before it had been customary to take to picnics. Out of one basket came a snow-white table-cloth and napkins; out of another, a chafing-dish, a loaf of home-made brown bread, and a couple of pats of delicious Darlington butter. A third basket revealed a large loaf of "Election Cake," with a thick sugary frosting; a fourth was full of crisp little jumbles, made after an old family recipe and warranted to melt in the mouth. There was a pile of thin, beautifully cut sandwiches; plenty of light-buttered rolls; and a cold fowl, ready carved into portions. By the time that these provisions were unpacked, Maud and Georgie were seen descending the hill at a rapid walk, which, at sight of the festive preparations below, changed to what Julia Prime called "a hungry gallop." By this time exercise and fresh air had made everybody so desperately hungry that it seemed impossible to wait another moment; so, while Mrs. Gray heated the coffee and dropped the large pink potatoes into their bed of embers to roast, the younger members of the party fell to work on the sandwiches, just to take off the fine edge of their appetites till something better was ready.

When the coffee was hot, Mrs. Gray seated herself by the rock, lit the lamp under her chafing-dish, dropped in a bit of butter, sprinkled with pepper and salt, and proceeded to "scramble" a great dish of eggs. Did any of you ever eat hot scrambled eggs under a tree when you were furiously hungry? If not, you can form no idea of the pleasure which the "Early Dippers" took in theirs. But it was not the eggs only; it was everything: never was a luncheon so delicious, the girls protested. New potatoes roasted in the ashes were a feast for the gods; and as for the grandmother's cake with which the repast wound up, it baffled analysis and description.

Mrs. Gray had made this cake with her own hands, "in order to carry out the historic verities," as she said. It used to be part of the religion of New England, especially of Connecticut, she explained; and she told them how once, when she was a girl, making a visit to an old aunt in Wethersfield, she had sat up nearly all night over a "raising" of Election cake.

"But why did you do that?" asked the girls.

"Well, you see, my aunt had a sudden attack of rheumatism in her arm. She was going to have the sewing-society meet at her house; and such a thing as a sewing-society without Election cake was not to be dreamed of. So I offered to make it; and I was bound that it should be good. The peculiarity of this particular cake is that it must rise twice before it is baked. You mix half the butter and sugar, and so on, with the yeast; and when that is light, you put in the other half. Now, my first half refused to rise."

"What did you do?"

"Oh, I sat beside it with one of Scott's novels, and I waited. It was rather poky; for my aunt and her servant had gone to bed, and there were queer creaks and noises now and then, as there always are in old houses. Midnight struck, and one, and two, before the first bubbles appeared on the surface of the cake; and I had fallen asleep over my book more than once, before I could be quite sure that it was safe to stir in the remainder of the spice and fruit, and go to bed. It was just four o'clock when I finally put out my lamp; and very sleepy I was next day, as you may imagine: but the cake turned out a great success, and I had many compliments about it from the crack housekeepers in the neighborhood, when they found that it was of my making."

"Wasn't it a dreadful trouble to have to make cake and things like that at home?" asked Maud Hallett. "I think I would rather have had it not quite so good, and got it from the confectioner's, than to have all that fuss and bother."

"My dear, there were no confectioners in those days except in two or three of the largest cities, and none even then who would be thought worth speaking of in our time. It was a case of home-made cake or none; and though it was certainly a great deal of trouble, the cake was better than any confectioner's cake that I ever tasted. People took great pride in it; and recipes were copied and handed about and talked over with an interest which would be impossible now-a-days, when everything comes to hand ready made, and you can order a loaf of sponge cake by postal card, and have it appear in a few hours, sent by express from central New York, as some of us have been doing this summer."

The last crumb of the Grandmother's loaf had now disappeared, and Mrs. Gray proposed that the girls should go for a scramble on the hills while she repacked the baskets. But this division of labor was not permitted. The girls insisted that they must be allowed to stay and help, and that the scramble would be no fun at all without their matron. Julia seized the coffee-pot and chafing-dish, and ran up the hill to rinse them at the spring; the others collected forks and plates; and, many hands making light work, in a very short while all was in order, and Mrs. Gray in readiness to head the walking party.

She guided them to the top of the granite ridge which is visible from Newport, and made them observe the peculiarity of the rock lines, and the contrast between their bareness and the fertility of the little intervening glades, for which they serve as a natural conservatory. Then they dipped down into the thickets of the farther side, finding all manner of ferns and wild-flowers and shy growing things, and so to the sandy flats above the third beach, with their outlook across the river-like strait to Little Compton and up the curving shore of Newport Island, set with old farm-houses and solemn orchards of gnarled apple-trees. From thence a short walk brought them to the end of the ridge and to Bishop Berkeley's seat, with its ponderous projecting roof of rocks; and they all sat down to rest just where he is said to have sat with his books and pen, looking off toward far Bermuda, and dreaming of the "star of empire." At that time no ugly brick chimneys or artificial water-basin existed to mar the foreground; and nothing sweeter or more peaceful could be imagined than the view from the rocky shelf,—the breadth of ocean lit with clear sun, the shining capes to right and left, the yellow sand-dunes and winding creek bordered with brown grasses and patches of mallow or green rushes, and over all the arch of blue summer sky. One or two carriages rolled along the distant road as they sat there; but otherwise; the stillness was unbroken save by the twitter of birds in the woods behind them, the chirp of sand-peeps or the scream of gulls on the beach, and the soft intermittent boom of the surf.

It had been a perfect afternoon, and a great success, all the picnickers voted, as they parted in the dusk on the gravel-walk in front of Mrs. Gray's door. Yet, after all, there was much to be said for Newport and civilization, and they were not sorry to come back to them. It was all very well to play at being old-fashioned for a day; but modern times have their distinct charms and conveniences, and if the girls, on sober second-thought, preferred their own share of the centuries to any other, no one need count them blameworthy.

CHAPTER VIII.
BRIC-A-BRAC.

ONE afternoon in August, Candace happened to be alone in the drawing-room with Mrs. Gray when Mrs. Joy was announced.

"My dear," began that lady, after administering the two hard, rapid little kisses which were her idea of a cordial greeting, "I've come to see if you don't want to go down to the Point with me. There's an old woman there, I hear, who has a lot of wonderful old china and some mahogany arm-chairs which she wants to sell, and I'm going to look at them. Do put your things on, and come. I hate to drive alone; and there's no fun in this sort of expedition unless there's some one along with you."

"You are very kind," said Mrs. Gray; "but I have promised Mr. Gray to go with him at four to call on some friends who have just arrived at Bateman's, so it's quite impossible for me to go with you. Who is the old woman? Do you recollect her name?"

"Oh, Collishan or Collisham,—some name like that. She lives in Third Street."

"It must be old Miss Colishaw. Are you sure she wants to sell her china?" asked Mrs. Gray, who as a child had spent many summers in Newport before it became a fashionable

150

watering-place, and knew the townspeople much better than did Mrs. Joy.

"I believe so; why shouldn't she? She's as poor as a church mouse, they tell me; and what use can such things be to her? She would rather have the money, of course. You can't go, then? I'm awfully sorry. But you'll let me have one of the girls, dear, won't you? I absolutely can't do it alone."

"Georgie has gone to drive with Berry, and I am sorry to say that Gertrude is on the sofa with a headache."

"Well, here's Miss Candace; she hasn't a headache, I'm sure: perhaps she will take pity on me.—You'll come, won't you? that's a dear. Run and put on your hat. It's a splendid afternoon, and the Point's a very interesting place if you happen to like old things. I don't care for them myself; but they're all the fashion now, you know, and I dare say you've caught the fever with the rest of the folks.—She can come, can't she, dear Mrs. Gray?"

"I don't think she has any engagement," replied Mrs. Gray, trying not to smile at the struggle with dismay that was going on in Candace's countenance; "she likes driving, and it is a beautiful afternoon.—You can go, can't you, Cannie?"

It was impossible on the spur of the moment to frame any excuse. Mrs. Joy's eyes were full upon her; Cousin Kate gave no help; there seemed nothing to do but to comply. Candace murmured something about "Certainly,—very kind,—very happy," and went away to put on the red hat, which went very well with the dress of red and white linen that she happened to have on. It was a new one, which Mrs. Gray had bought for warm days, and which Elizabeth had fitted and made. She wore a red rose in her breast, and had a pair of gray gloves, and she looked very fresh and girlish in this simple costume; but Mrs. Joy did not quite approve of it.

"Why don't they fix the little thing up better?" she was thinking to herself as she got into the carriage. "It's too bad. She'd be quite nice-looking if she were a little more stylish. A light silk, now, or a surah in two shades, like Berry's blue, would make quite a different thing of her."

"You've been down on the Point before now, I suppose," she said as they rolled smoothly along the Avenue.

"Yes, once I did. Cousin Kate took me with her one day to call on a friend of hers, Miss Gisborne."

"Oh, yes, that queer old maid. I know they're very intimate, though I confess I never could see what Mrs. Gray finds in her to like. She's so eccentric, and so different from other people, and she wears such extraordinary clothes."

"But she's very nice, and she tells the funniest stories, and her house is ever so pretty," said Candace, rather at a loss to know what she ought to say.

"Ah, indeed, is it? Inside, you mean. I don't think it amounts to much outside, though people who have a mania for old houses rave about it, I believe. I'm afraid

I'm dreadfully modern in my tastes. I can't, for the life of me, see any beauty in ceilings so low that you bump your head against them, and little scraps of windows filled with greenish glass that you can't see through, and which make you look like a mouldy fright, if any one looks through from the outside."

"Miss Gisborne's window-panes are green," admitted Candace. "Some of them are so old that they have colors all over them like mother-of-pearl,—red and blue and yellow. I liked to see them; and she told us that last summer an architect who was going by the house stopped and looked at them a long time, and then rang the bell and offered to give her new sashes with great big panes in them if she would exchange; but she wouldn't."

"The more fool she!" rejoined Mrs. Joy, frankly. "My! what a splendid big house that is going to be! That's the kind of thing I like." And she pointed to an enormous half-finished structure of wood, painted pumpkin color and vermilion, which with its size, its cottage-like details, and the many high thin chimneys which rose above its towering roofs, looked a happy mixture of an asylum, a factory, and a Swiss châlet.

"But what a little bit of ground there is about it for such a big house!" said Candace, whose country eyes were often struck by the disproportion between the Newport edifices and the land on which they stood.

"Yes; land is so dreadfully dear now that people can't afford large places."

"I wonder why this is called 'Farewell Street,'" said Candace, looking at the name painted on the corner of a street into which they were turning.

"Some people say it's because this is the street by which funerals come away from the Cemetery," replied Mrs. Joy. "There's the Reading-room down there. You've seen that, I suppose. Mrs. Gray comes down to the mothers' meetings sometimes, I know."

"Yes; and she has promised to take me with her some day, but we haven't gone yet."

The carriage now turned into a narrow street, parallel with the Bay, but not in sight of it; and Mrs. Joy indicated to her footman a low dormer-windowed house, shabby with weather-stains and lack of paint, whose only ornament was a large and resplendent brass knocker on its front door.

"That's the place," she said. "Just look at that knocker. I know for a certainty that lots of people have offered to buy it, and the absurd old creature to whom it belongs won't sell. She declares that it's been there ever since she can remember, and that it shall stay there as long as she stays. So ridiculous, when things of the kind bring such an enormous price now, and she really needs the money!"

The carriage now stopped. Mrs. Joy got out, and Candace with her. The footman seized the shining knocker, and gave a loud rap.

"Go back to the carriage, Wilkins," said Mrs. Joy. Then she added in a low voice to Candace: "Get close to the door, dear. These people are so queer. I often have to push my way in, but I can always manage them in the end."

The door was opened a very little way by a very little girl.

"Is Miss Collisham at home?" asked Mrs. Joy, at the same time inserting her foot deftly between the door and the door-frame, to insure that the door should not be closed against her.

"No, 'm," said the child. "She's gone out."

"Dear me, what a shame! where is she?" demanded the visitor, in an aggrieved tone, as if Miss Colishaw had no right to be out when wanted by the owner of such a fine equipage.

"She's over to old Miss Barnes's. She's sick," replied the little girl.

"Who's sick?—old Miss Barnes? And where does she live?"

"Just over there in First Street," said the child, staring at Candace, whose big red hat had caught her fancy. "'Tain't but a little way," she added.

"Ah, indeed!" said Mrs. Joy, pushing her way into the entry. "Well, then, you just run over to this place, dear, and tell Miss Collisham that there's a lady waiting to speak to her on business. Be quick, that's a good little girl! This young lady and I will sit down here and wait till you come back."

The small maiden looked uncertain and rather frightened; but Mrs. Joy marched resolutely into the little parlor on one side of the hall, and seated herself; so, after a pause of hesitation, the child seized a sun-bonnet which lay on a chair, and set off at a run in the direction indicated. The moment she was gone Mrs. Joy jumped briskly up.

"Such a piece of good luck!" she cried. "One so rarely gets the chance to examine a place like this without the bother of a family standing by to watch everything you do." Then, to Candace's horror and astonishment, she walked straight across the room to a cupboard which her experienced eye had detected in the side of the chimney, opened the door, and took a survey of the contents.

"Nothing there," she remarked, locking it up, "only medicine bottles and trash. Let's try again." She opened a closet door, and emitted a sigh of satisfaction.

"These must be the very plates I heard of," she said. "Let me see,—five, six, eight,—a complete dozen, I declare, and all in good order,—and a platter, and two dishes! Well, this is a find; and such lovely china, too,—I must have it. Mrs. Kinglake's,—that she's so proud of—isn't half so handsome;

and she has only eight plates. Now, where are those chairs that they told me about, I wonder?"

Candace was sitting in one of the very chairs, as it proved; the other Mrs. Joy presently discovered in a little back-room which opened from the parlor, and which she lost no time in rummaging. She had just unlocked another closet door, and was standing before it with a pitcher in her hand, when the mistress of the house appeared,—a tall, thin, rather severe-looking woman, whose cheeks still wore the fresh color which cheeks retain till old age in the Narragansett country.

Candace, who had remained in her chair in a state of speechless and helpless dismay, watching Mrs. Joy's proceedings through the open door, saw her coming, but had no time to warn Mrs. Joy.

"You wanted to see me on business?" said Miss Colishaw, fixing a pair of wrathful eyes on Mrs. Joy, the pitcher, and the open door of the closet.

"Oh, is it Miss Collisham?" replied that lady, neither noticing nor caring for the very evident indignation of look and tone. "Your little girl was so kind as to say that she would go and call you; and while we were waiting we thought we would look at this curious old—"

"We! are there more of you, then?" demanded Miss Colishaw, glaring into the closet as if she expected to see other audacious visitors concealed in its depths. Finding none, she closed the door and turned its stout wooden button with a good deal of energy.

"If you've any business with me, ma'am," she said, "perhaps you'll be so kind as to step into the parlor and say what it is."

"Certainly," responded Mrs. Joy, airily. "But before we go do tell me about this curious old jug. It's Spode, is it not? I'm almost sure that it must be Spode, or some other of the very old English wares. Do you know about it?"

"I know that it was my mother's yeast-pitcher, and that's all that I care to know," replied Miss Colishaw, grimly, taking it out of her hand. "I use it to keep corks in."

"Corks! How amusing! But it's really a nice old piece, you know. I'd like to buy it if you don't care any more for it than that. You could put your corks in something else just as well."

"It ain't for sale," said Miss Colishaw, decidedly, putting the pitcher again into the closet, and leading the way into the parlor.

Candace, who had heard all, and was feeling awkward and guilty to the last degree, rose as they entered, and courtesied to Miss Colishaw. Perhaps her face showed something of the shame and annoyance with which her heart was filled; for Miss Colishaw's iron expression relaxed a little, and the "Good-afternoon" she vouchsafed her sounded a shade less implacable.

"Oh, I forgot!" said Mrs. Joy, turning back to the rear room. "There's this old chair, Miss Collisham."

"Colishaw's my name," interposed her hostess.

"I beg your pardon, I'm sure; so it is, of course. Well, as I was saying, I noticed a delightful old arm-chair in this room,—ah, there it is! It exactly matches some without arms which I bought at Sypher's. If you'd like to part with this and the other in the front room, Miss—Miss Collishall, I should be glad to buy them; and I'd give you a very good price for them because of the match."

Miss Colishaw made no answer.

"Then there's some china that I observed in another closet," went on Mrs. Joy, returning again to the parlor, and opening the door of the closet in question. "This red and blue, I mean. I see you have a good deal of it, and it's a kind I particularly fancy. It's like some which my dear old grandmother used to have." Mrs. Joy's tone became quite sentimental. "I'd give almost anything for it, for the sake of old associations. I wish you'd fix a price on this, Miss Collisham."

"Very well, then, I will,—one million of dollars," replied Miss Colishaw, losing all command over her temper. "No, ma'am, I'm not joking. One million of dollars!—not a cent less; and not even that would pay me for my mother's china, and the chair my father used to sit in when he was old. They ain't for sale; and when I've said that once, I've said it for always."

"But, my dear Miss Collishall—"

"I ain't your dear, and my name ain't Collishall. Colishaw's what I'm called; and it's a good old Newport name, though you don't seem to be able to remember it."

"I beg your pardon," said Mrs. Joy, loftily. "It's rather an unusual name, and I never happened to hear it till to-day. Then you don't care to sell any of these old things?"

"No, ma'am, not one thing."

"Well, I must say that I consider you very foolish. This sort of old stuff won't always be the fashion; and the minute the fashion goes out, they won't be worth anything. Nobody will want to buy them."

"They'll be worth just the same to me then that they are now," responded Miss Colishaw, more gently. She evidently saw the hopelessness of trying to impress her point of view on Mrs. Joy.

"I dare say you have an attic-full of delightful old spinning-wheels and things," remarked that lady, quick to mark the change of tone and hoping to profit by it. She glanced toward the stair-foot as she spoke. Miss Colishaw quickly stepped in front of the stairs, and stood there with the air of an ancient Roman defending his household gods.

"Yes, ma'am, I have an attic," she said dryly. "It's a very good attic, and it's stuffed full of old things. There's a fender and two pairs of fire-dogs—"

Mrs. Joy's eyes sparkled. "Oh, do let us go up and see it!" she cried.

"No, you don't!" said Miss Colishaw, taking a firmer grasp of the baluster. "There's a wool-wheel, and a flax-wheel, and a winder, and three warming-pans—"

"Dear me! What a delightful place!" put in Mrs. Joy.

"There's lots and lots of old truck," continued the implacable Miss Colishaw. "It all belonged to my mother and my grandmother and her mother before her. It's all up there; and there it's going to stay, if all the rich ladies in Newport come down to try to wheedle me out of it. Not a soul of them shall set foot in my attic."

"Well, I must say that I think you very foolish," said Mrs. Joy, settling the wrists of her long gloves. "You're very poor, and these old things are no use to you in the way you live; and you'd far better take the money they would bring, and make yourself comfortable."

Miss Colishaw was now pale with anger.

"And who told you I was poor?" she demanded. "Did I ever come a-begging to you? Did I ever walk into your house to pry and rummage, and tell you that your things were no use? When I do you'll have a right to come here and behave as you have, but not a minute before. Use! They are of use.

They remind me of my family,—of the time I was young, when we all lived in this house together, before Newport grew to be a fashionable boarding-place and was spoiled for people of the old sort. If that's all the business you have with me, madam, I think we have got through with it."

"Really, there's no occasion for being so very rude," said Mrs. Joy.

"Rude!" Miss Colishaw gave an acrid laugh. "Mine ain't fashionable manners, I know; but I guess they're about as good." She opened the front door, and held it suggestively wide. Mrs. Joy swept through.

"Come, Miss Arden," she called back over her shoulder.

Candace could do nothing but look as apologetic as she felt. "I'm so sorry," she murmured, as she passed Miss Colishaw.

"You haven't done anything. It's she who ought to be sorry," returned Miss Colishaw, and banged the door behind her as she passed through.

"What a horrid old person!" said Mrs. Joy, who looked heated and vexed. "I never met any one so impertinent. And such a fool, too! Why, she takes in sewing, I am told, or makes cake,—some of those things. She's as poor as Job's turkey; yet there she sits, with those valuable things absolutely wasting in her poky old house, and refuses to sell them. I wish I had spoken more strongly to her! I declare, I've a good mind to go back and do it now. It is such perfect folly. She really ought to be reasoned out of it."

"Oh, I wouldn't," urged Candace,—"I wouldn't go back. She was so angry. I don't know what she would say if you did."

"My dear, I don't care a red cent what she says. All the old women on the Point can't frighten me," declared Mrs. Joy. She reflected a little; then she gave up her intention.

"After all, it isn't worth the trouble. She's just that sort of obstinate old creature who will never listen to a word of advice. I knew, the moment I looked at her, that nothing I could say would do any good. Generally I can turn that kind of person round my finger. Why, you'd be surprised if I told you of the bargains I have got out of old garrets over on Conanicut and down the Island. But, really and truly, I'm a little tired of it; and I never did care much for such old duds, except that other people have them and it is the thing to have them. I'd rather go to Howard's any day, and get a lot of nice French china. Howard has such exquisite things always."

So the carriage was ordered to Coddington's Cove; and as they rolled smoothly past the Maitland Woods, neither Mrs. Joy nor Candace guessed that at that moment Miss Colishaw was sitting in her little back-room, with the old yeast-pitcher in her lap, crying as if her heart would break.

"It's bad enough to be old and poor and alone in the world," she sobbed to herself, "without having fine stuck-up folks coming right in to sauce you out of your senses." She wiped her eyes, and looked for a minute at the pitcher.

"Betsey Colishaw, you're a fool!" she remarked aloud. "You might have kept your temper. The woman didn't hurt you any. And there was that young thing looking so kind of sorry. You might have said a pleasant word to her, anyhow, even if you were all riled up with the other."

On sped the carriage, the lovely Upper Bay always in sight, until on the curve of the long Coddington's Point it turned, and retraced its course so as to strike Washington Street at the lower end. It was a delicious afternoon. The tide was flowing freshly in, and the brisk northwest breeze which met it sent little white-caps dancing all over the surface. Crafts of all kinds were traversing the harbor: yachts and cat-boats were out in numbers; schooners and barges sped up the bay, their sails shining against the green Island shores; row-boats and steam-tugs were crossing and recrossing between the city and the Fort and Torpedo Station. A sharp double whistle announced the "Eolus" just started on her up trip, with a long wake of creamy foam behind her. Fleets of white clouds were drifting across the sky, which was bluer than the sea, like ships of heaven, simulating and repeating the movements of those of earth below. Every wharf and dock was full of people, fishing, idling, or preparing to go out in boats. It was one of the moments when all mankind seems to be a-pleasuring, and to have laid aside all memory of the labors and the pains of this work-a-day world.

Mrs. Joy probably felt that she owed Candace some compensation for the unpleasant quarter of an hour which she had led her into at Miss Colishaw's; for she did her best to be entertaining, and to tell everything that she herself knew about Washington Street and its notabilities. She pointed out the two pretty old houses which have been so cleverly modernized into comfort without any sacrifice of their quaint exteriors; and the other and still finer one, once belonging to the Hunter family, whose renovations have gone so far toward spoiling it.

"It used to have a nice old staircase with a broad landing, and windows over the water, and beautiful mahogany balusters," explained Mrs. Joy. "But they've spoiled all that. They have painted over the elegant satinwood and old cherry wainscotings, and taken out the secret staircase; and now it's no better than any other square house with that kind of roof."

"Was there a secret staircase?" cried Candace. "Oh, what a pity they took it out! I always thought I should like to see one so much."

"I don't believe this would have interested you particularly. It was only a kind of narrow back-stairs, which was not commonly used. They do say, though, that ghosts used to be heard running up and down it quite often."

"Ghosts! How strange! What sort of noise did they make? I suppose no one ever saw them."

"One lady did."

"Really!" Candace's eyes were wide with attention.

"Yes. She was a friend of mine, and she used to board in the house before it was altered. She heard the noises, which were a sort of scratching and rustling, and she resolved to see what the ghost was like; so she took a candle and followed it downstairs."

"How brave! And what was it like?"

"It was like—a rat! When she caught sight of it, it was sitting on the edge of a pot of lard. It was picking its teeth, she said."

"A pot of lard!"

"Yes. The secret staircase led down to a sort of cellar, you see."

"Oh, Mrs. Joy, how disappointing!"

"I'm afraid ghost stories generally do turn out disappointing in the end. Here we are, close to old Fort Greene. Would you like to jump out, and run down to the water's edge and see it?"

"Oh, thank you, I should like it ever so much."

It was but a few steps from the carriage to the grassy top of the old redoubt; but when Cannie had picked her way down the steep incline toward the shore, she found herself entirely out of sight of the street and the houses, out of sight of everything except the lovely sunlit Bay which stretched before her. There was no sound except the plash of the waves, and for a moment she felt as much alone as if she had been in the depths of a country solitude. Then another sound came vaguely to her ear,—a low murmur of conversation; and she became aware that the Fort held other visitors besides herself. A rock hid the speakers from her, whoever they might be; the voices were too indistinct for recognition, and it was accident rather than intention which led her to diverge from the path, as she returned to the carriage, in a manner which gave her a view of the party.

There were three persons,—a man and two girls. The man was young and good-looking; he was also well dressed, but there was something about him which, even to Candace's inexperience, suggested the idea that he was not quite a gentleman. One of the girls was standing with her back to Candace, talking eagerly in a hushed voice; the other sat on a stone in an attitude of troubled dejection. Her face was in shadow; but she turned a little as Candace passed, and to her wondering surprise she saw that it was no other than her cousin Georgie Gray.

CHAPTER IX.
PERPLEXED.

CANDACE paused for a second, surprised and hesitating; then she walked on again. Georgie had not seemed to observe her. The other girl was doubtless Berry Joy, with whom she was less at ease than with anybody else. She felt not the least desire to confront her, and a strange man to boot; besides, Mrs. Joy must not be kept waiting.

"That looks like Berry's village cart," exclaimed Mrs. Joy, as they drove past a side street where a little vehicle stood drawn up in the shade under the care of a natty groom. "Was that James and the cart, Wilkins?"

"Yes, ma'am, I believe it was."

"I wonder where the girls can be," continued Mrs. Joy. "At the Parishes', most likely, taking afternoon tea. That's a very favorite place at sunset with all the young people. There is such a wide piazza, and a splendid view." Having said this, she dismissed the subject from her mind.

They lingered so long in Thames Street, over various errands, that it was nearly dinner-time before Candace reached home. Georgie was there before her; she still had her bonnet on, and was sitting on the piazza with her mother and Gertrude, giving an account of her afternoon.

"And then we drove down to the Old Point, and called on the Parishes," she concluded; "and, mamma, as we came away Miss Gisborne saw us from her window, and called out that I was to tell you that Mr.—somebody—Card—Caird—some Englishman, at all events—was coming to-morrow, and would you please be sure to lunch with her on Wednesday and meet him?"

"Caird, the artist? yes, I know. Miss Gisborne was expecting him."

Georgie seemed to have finished her narrative. She had not said a word about Fort Greene.

"Now, Candace, what are your adventures?" demanded Gertrude. "It is quite exciting, after a dull afternoon on the sofa, to have you all come in and tell me what you have been about. I watched you drive away with a face like a frightened kitten."

"You would have seen me looking a great deal more frightened if you had been with us at Miss Colishaw's," said Candace; and she proceeded to relate what had happened, in a quiet, demure way which was particularly funny, throwing in a little unconscious mimicry which made the scene real to her audience. Miss Colishaw's grim indignation, Mrs. Joy's cool audacity, her own compunctious helplessness,—all were indicated in turn. Before she had done, they were in fits of indignant laughter.

"Well, really, I did not think even Mrs. Joy could behave so outrageously as that," remarked Gertrude.

"It is really too bad," said Mrs. Gray. "Miss Colishaw is one of the salt of the earth, always working herself to death for anybody who is sick or in trouble, or poorer than herself. I am afraid her feelings were really hurt. She is sensitive about her poverty, and has a great regard for her old family relics. I feared that there might be some mistake about her wishing to sell her china when Mrs. Joy spoke about it; but it is a long time since I saw the old lady, and I thought it possible that something had occurred to make her glad of the money. I am really shocked at Mrs. Joy."

"If only I could have seen her at the cupboard, with the yeast-pitcher in her hand, and Miss Colishaw's face!" cried Gertrude, with another burst of laughter. "Well, after this truly awful interview what did you do next, Candace?"

"We drove to Coddington's Cove, and then we came back to Washington Street, and Mrs. Joy told me about the old houses; and then she stopped the carriage by old Fort Greene, and I went down to the shore to look at it."

"Did you?" said Georgie with sudden interest; "why—why, Berry and I were there too. We ran down for a moment."

"I thought I saw you," said Candace, simply.

She was looking straight at Georgie as she spoke, and was surprised to see her flush suddenly, and then turn as suddenly pale. Her change of color was so marked that her mother could scarcely have failed to notice it, had her attention not been for the moment occupied by Frederic, who just brought out a note which required an answer. Gertrude was looking another way; only Candace noticed Georgie's unwonted emotion. Nothing more was said about Fort Greene at the time; but a little later, when she was in her room smoothing her hair for dinner, Georgie tapped at the door.

"Cannie," she said, "I'm going to ask you not to say anything more to anybody about having seen Berry and me on Washington Street to-day."

"Certainly, I won't," replied Candace, making in her surprise one of those hasty promises which are so often repented of afterward; "but why not?"

"Oh, well, there are no very important reasons; it's just that I would rather you wouldn't."

"Very well." But Candace felt vaguely dissatisfied with this explanation, and a little curious.

She thought of this promise, and of Georgie's odd manner of exacting it from her, as she fell asleep that night, and again the next morning; but gradually it faded from her mind, until, about ten days later, something occurred to revive the remembrance. Mrs. Joy called to ask two of the girls to drive with Berry and herself to see the polo play. Gertrude happened to be out; so Candace fell heir to her share of the invitation. Mrs. Gray was glad to have her go. She herself did not often visit the Polo Ground, and she thought Candace would enjoy seeing a match, and that it would be something pleasant for her to remember.

The Polo Ground is a large enclosure to the south of Spring Street, and well out of the town. It is shut in by a high paling, built with the intention of excluding every one who does not pay for the pleasure of witnessing the game. Nature, however,—that free-handed dame,—has frustrated this precaution by providing, close to the paling, a little rocky bluff, or rise of land, not owned by the Polo Association, whose top commands a clear view over the fence; and on polo days this point of vantage is usually well filled by on-lookers of an impecunious description. There was quite a little crowd on the brow of "Deadhead Hill," as it is called, when Mrs. Joy's carriage turned in at the gates; and she glanced that way and said, "It is really too bad about that hill!" in a dissatisfied tone, as if the enjoyment of these non-subscribers jarred in some way, or interfered with the pleasure for which she herself was forced to pay a round price.

Inside the gate appeared a large railed enclosure, with a wicket at either end; and about this carriages full of gay people were drawn up in rows, two or three abreast. The ponies which were to be used in the game were being led up and down on the farther side of the ground, where was a range of out-buildings. Presently a bell rang. There was a little confusion of unblanketing and mounting, and eight riders armed with long mallets rode forward. Four wore red caps, and four blue; and the two colors ranged themselves opposite each other at the wickets. The umpire tossed a little ball into the middle of the ground, and the game began.

Candace was at first rather inclined to laugh at the riders, who were so much too tall for their little steeds that in some cases their legs seemed in danger of hitting the ground; but before long she had become so interested in the game and the bold riding that she no longer felt inclined to laugh. The object of each side was to drive the ball through its own wicket; and to effect this a great deal of both courage and skill were required, not only on the part of the horsemen, but of the ponies as well. More than once all the eight seemed to be collected in a breathless tangle about and above the ball, crowding, pushing, struggling for the chance at a stroke; and in such cases the ponies seemed to divide the excitement with their masters, and fenced and curved and described indescribably short circles, regardless of the danger of getting a hard rap from the cruel mallets on their own poor little hoofs. Then, when some lucky hit sent the ball spinning across the ground, it was quite beautiful to see the alacrity with which the little creatures, of their own accord, as it were, rushed, after it, obeying the slightest indication from rein or spur, and apparently measuring the distance and the opportunities as accurately as their riders. The beat of their small hoofs on the smooth ground was so swift and even that it was more like a rustle than a rush. To and fro flew the ball, now almost at the blue wicket, then reached and sent back in the very nick of time by one of the red champions. Candace was so fascinated that she had no eyes for any one else till, turning her head by accident, her eye lighted upon a face in the crowd near the carriage; and with a flash of recognition she knew that it was the stranger of whom she had caught that momentary glimpse at Fort Greene. Involuntarily she glanced at Berry Joy and Georgie, and perceived that the former had seen the man also and was trying to look as if she had not seen him, while the latter was honestly unconscious. There was something odd about the man's manner, which kept Candace's attention fixed. He seemed to be standing carelessly among other spectators watching the game, and yet by a series of dexterous movements and small shiftings of position he was gradually edging toward the carriage. Presently a forward step more decided than the rest brought him close to it. Georgie saw him now. A deep color flushed her face; she lowered her parasol as if to hide it.

"I believe you dropped this, madam," said the man, stooping suddenly as if to pick something up from the ground, and handing to Berry what seemed to be a note.

"Oh, thanks!" said Berry, in a confused voice, quite different from her ordinary voice.

The stranger raised his hat formally, and moved aside.

"What was that?" asked Mrs. Joy, who had been watching the game and had seen nothing of this by-play. "Did you drop something, Berry?"

"Only a note from Julia Prime," answered Berry, slipping the paper in her pocket.

"It was very civil of that person, whoever he was," said Mrs. Joy, unsuspiciously.

Berry and Georgie exchanged looks. Candace was at a loss what to think.

There are few better keepers of secrets than shy people. They do not let things out by accident, as talkative persons do; it is easier for them to be silent than to talk, to keep counsel than to betray it. But apart from being shy, Candace's instincts were honorable. She had a lady-like distaste of interfering with other people's affairs or seeming to pry into them. She said not a word to any one about this matter of the Polo Ground, and she tried not to think about it; although it was not in human nature not to feel a little curiosity, and she caught herself observing Georgie rather more than usual, though without intending it.

This quickened observation showed her two things: first, that Georgie had something on her mind; and secondly, that she was determined not to show it. She laughed and talked rather more than was her custom; and if the laughter was a little forced, no one else seemed to find it out. There were times when Candace almost persuaded herself that the whole thing was the effect of her own imagination, which had exaggerated something that was perfectly commonplace into importance simply because she did not understand it; and then again she doubted, and was sure that Georgie was not like her usual self.

So another week went by, and brought them to September. There was no sign of autumn as yet. Every leaf was as green and fresh on its bough, every geranium as bright on its stalk, as if summer were just beginning instead of just ended. But with the presage which sends the bird southward long before the cold is felt, and teaches the caterpillar to roll its cocoon and the squirrel to make ready its winter's nest and store of nuts, the gay summer crowd began to melt away. Every day brought a lessened list of arrivals at the hotels; and already there was that sense of a season over and done with and about to be laid up and shelved for the winter, which all watering-places know so well, and which is as a nipping frost to the hopes of landlords and letters of lodgings. Just why "Finis" should be written so early on the fair page of the Newport season, it is hard to explain; for, charming as is the summer, September and October are more charming still, and nowhere does the later autumn exhibit a more indulgent mood, holding back the winter till the last possible moment, and sometimes coaxing summer to aid and abet with supplies of greenery and flowers, till the New Year comes to put an end to the merry game.

Mr. Gray began to go to town in the Sunday-night boat for two or three days of business, though he still spent the larger half of the week in Newport. Marian was sent to Lenox for a week's visit to an aunt. The family seemed very small now; and when Mrs. Gray one Monday morning announced her intention of running up to Boston next day for the night and taking Gertrude with her, Georgie loudly protested.

"It is really cruel of you, mamma. Cannie and I will feel like two deserted little scraps, all alone in this big house. I do think you might wait till papa is at home. And there's Marian coming back to-morrow night. What on earth shall we do with her all day? She will feel dreadfully to find you gone."

"I am sorry about Marian," confessed Mrs. Gray; "but Tuesday happens to be the best day for us on several accounts. You and Candace must be particularly good to her, and not let her feel aggrieved or forlorn. I have ordered the breakfasts and luncheons and dinner for to-morrow and Wednesday, so you will have no housekeeping to trouble you, and we shall be back at six o'clock, you know. Two days are but a short time, after all. You might ask a couple of girls to dine with you to-morrow,—any one you like."

But Georgie seemed out of spirits. She was dull and dreamy, and said she didn't care to invite anybody,—she would rather have a nice lazy time by themselves, if Candace liked it just as well. Candace, who had made up her mind to the inevitable Berry Joy, was glad to be let off; so she spent a very quiet day, for Georgie went to her room as soon as lunch was over, to lie down, as she said, and sleep off a little headache, and Candace was left alone till nearly dinner-time.

Marian's arrival from the train brought a little stir and variety; but it was not of the most pleasurable kind, for she was so disappointed and indignant at finding her mother absent, that till the first sharp sting of vexation had abated, nothing could be got out of her but sobs and broken words of complaint. Even when she grew calmer, things were still rather melancholy; for she was too tired and depressed for speech, and just sat in silence, leaning her head against Candace's shoulder until bedtime. Nor did Georgie and Candace find much to say to each other after she had departed. Georgie remarked, rather peevishly, that Marian was a most cross, tiresome child sometimes, and Candace said, "Yes, poor little thing! but she was really very tired this time, as well as cross;" then each took a book and read to herself till ten o'clock, when they separated with a brief good-night. It was a great contrast to the usual bright, cheerful evenings of the household; and Cannie, as she undressed, was conscious of being low-spirited. "Homesick" she would have called it; but the phrase did not justly express her mood, for even on that dull evening I am very sure that she did not pine for Aunt Myra, or for the North Tolland farm-house, which was the only place she had ever called by the name of home.

The next day opened more brightly. Marian was asked to lunch with the Frewens, who were her favorite friends; and her absence was something of a relief to the others. Georgie and Candace did their little morning tasks, not forgetting the arrangement of the fresh flowers, which usually fell to Gertrude's share; then Georgie sat down to practise, and Candace settled herself in a deep cushioned chair in the library with Motley's "Dutch Republic," which she was reading for the first time. It was the chapter on the siege of Leyden; and the wild, fantastic nocturne by Chopin which Georgie was playing, seemed to blend and mix itself with the tragic narrative. Candace did not know how long the reading and the music had been going on, each complementing the other. She was so absorbed in her book as not to heed the sound of the bell or Frederic's noiseless tread as he crossed the hall to answer it; but she roused from her absorption as the nocturne came suddenly to an end with a crash of startled chords, and Georgie's hands fell from the keys, at the sight of Berry Joy, who came hurriedly in at the door. Candace in her corner was invisible.

"Oh, Georgie, that dreadful creature is here again," she heard Berry say, while Georgie answered with a little despairing cry, "Not really! oh, Berry, what shall we do?"

Then came a long whispered confabulation; then another tinkle at the door-bell.

"Frederic, I am engaged," Georgie called out.—"Come upstairs, Berry. If we stay here, some one is certain to break in." The two rushed across the hall. Candace heard their rapid steps on the stairs; then Georgie's door shut with a bang, and all was still.

Her book dropped into her lap unheeded. Her mind was full of puzzled amazement. Who was the "dreadful creature," and what did it all mean?

The silence in the house was unbroken except by the tick-tick of the tall clock. It made her nervous at last, and she went out on the lawn to get rid of the sensation. She picked a few flowers, pulled the seed-pods from one of the geraniums under her care, and spent some minutes in petting and fondling Marian's pretty colly, who lay stretched out luxuriously in the full rays of the mild September sunshine. Then she caught a glimpse of Berry's figure passing out of the gate, and went back to the house. The drawing-room was empty. Motley lay on the floor where she had dropped him. She picked up the volume, and slowly mounted the stairs. As she passed through the upper entry she heard a sound from the morning-room; was it a sob? Candace gently approached the door. Again the sound came, an unmistakable sob; and looking in she saw Georgie, lying on her mother's sofa with her face hidden, sobbing as if her heart would break, and saying over and over to herself in a voice which was like a moan, "What shall I do? oh, what shall I do?"

CHAPTER X.
A WORD FITLY SPOKEN.

ALL Candace's timidity fled at the sight of Georgie's distress. She hurried across the room, knelt down by the sofa, and took her cousin's hand, which was as cold as a stone, between her own warm ones.

"What is it, Georgie? Don't cry so, Georgie, dear, please don't! Oh, what is the matter?" she said, in a voice so soft and affectionate and pleading, that it made its way straight to poor miserable Georgie's heart. She still sobbed; she still hid her face in the pillow; but she let Cannie hold her hand and stroke and kiss it, and seemed to find a little soothing in the kind touch and the tender words.

After a while the sobs grew fainter, and Georgie lay half exhausted, with her eyes shut, only now and then giving Cannie's hand a squeeze. Hers was one of those natures which cannot bear to suffer alone. Whatever was the matter, Georgie instinctively reached out for sympathy to the nearest source from which it could be had. Gertrude, her natural confidante, was away; and Candace, her sweet face full of pity and concern, was close at hand. Her touch felt warm and comforting; her tender voice was irresistible to Georgie's desolate mood. She turned her wet face with a sudden burst of gratitude and trust toward the little cousin whom she had till now held so cheaply, and who, at that moment, seemed the only friend left within reach.

"Cannie," she said, "I've a great mind to tell you—" Then she stopped.

Confidence is like a timid bird, which hops nearer and nearer to the hand that holds out a crumb, but all the while keeps its wings half poised for flight, should a gesture alarm it. Candace had the instinctive wisdom of a loving heart. She did not interrupt Georgie with a word; only her anxious eyes asked the questions which her tongue did not utter.

"I am in such trouble," said Georgie, thawing more and more under the influence of Cannie's silence and Cannie's look,—"in such a dreadful scrape! Oh, what will become of me?" wringing her hands. "You are so good, Cannie,—so kind. Will you promise not to breathe a word to anybody if I tell you all about it?"

"Yes," said Candace, "I promise."

"I know you can keep a secret," continued Georgie, sighing heavily; "you never said a word about that time at Fort Greene, yet I know you must have wondered what it all meant." A little pause; then she went on: "There really wasn't any harm in it when it began. It was last winter. One day Berry and I had been laughing over some of the 'Personals' in the 'Herald,' and just for fun we wrote one ourselves and sent it to the paper. It was an advertisement. We pretended it came from a lady who wanted to make the acquaintance of an eligible gentleman with a view to matrimony. We made it as ridiculous as we could, and we signed it 'Laura,' and said that all the answers could be sent to the Station D Post-office."

"And did you get any answers?"

"Oh, quantities! I never imagined that people could be so foolish. Why, there were a hundred and thirty the very first day, and ever so many afterward. Some of them were sentimental, and some of them were ridiculous, and some were really funny. I think the funny ones came from people who suspected that the advertisement was a hoax; but we got a great deal of amusement out of it, and we never for a moment dreamed that any one would suspect who put it in. Oh, how I wish we never had; for it brought that horrible man down upon us, and since then we have never had any peace of our lives."

"What horrible man?" asked Candace, more and more surprised.

"You saw him at Fort Greene. I don't know who he is myself, really. He says his name is James Alexander, but he tells such frightful lies that I don't believe it is his real name at all. He is a dreadful creature, and he has treated us so—" Georgie broke down into another fit of crying.

"But I don't understand," said Candace. "How could he treat you badly? How did he come to know you? What right had he to speak to you at all?"

"Oh, no right!" explained Georgie, quivering with sobs. "It was only that he found out about the advertisement, and then he frightened us. He suspected something, and hung about the post-office and watched, till one time when Berry and I went to get the 'Laura' letters. Then he followed us home, and found out where we both lived, and wrote to say that he had become possessed of our secret, and that he was a poor man in need of money, and if we would at once send him twenty-five dollars he would keep silent about it; but if not, he should feel bound to write to our friends, and let them know what we had been doing. We were both scared to death at this threat, and we made haste to send him the money, hoping that he would keep his word, and that we should never hear of him again. But we might have known better; for the very next week he wrote again, demanding fifty. And so it has gone on ever since. He never gives us any peace. We have to send him all he asks for, or else he declares he will call on papa, and not only tell him about the advertisement, but all sorts of horrible things which are not true at all. He won't believe that it was only to amuse ourselves that we sent the notice to the paper, and he hints the most dreadful things, and says papa and Mrs. Joy will be sure to believe him! Berry and I have grown so afraid that we would give a million, if we had it, to bribe him to go away and never let us hear from him again. But even that would be no use, for he would come back and demand another million," ended poor Georgie.

"And he actually comes up to Newport, and follows you about, and makes you give him money!" said Candace, horror-stricken at this glimpse of the hidden suffering endured by these two prosperous, cared-for girls, who were supposed to be without a sorrow in the world.

"Indeed, he does. He came that time when you saw him, the middle of August; and he wrote Berry a note to say that he must speak to us, and that if we didn't meet him somewhere, he should appeal to Mrs. Joy. We had to consent, of course, and we gave him all the money we had, and we thought he was gone; but just a few days after he appeared again on the Polo Ground, and handed Berry a note, which he pretended she had dropped out of the carriage. But it was really from himself; and he said that he had lost the money we gave him on a bet which had turned out badly, and he must have a hundred dollars more. You can't think how hard it has been for us to raise all this money, Cannie. Berry has her own income, but her mother likes to know what she does with it; and mamma chooses my things for me, so I don't have much of an allowance. We have been at our wits' end sometimes to know how to manage."

"And how did you?"

"Berry sold a diamond ring which she doesn't often wear, so her mother has not missed it, and I put in thirty dollars, which was all I had; and he went away, for good as we hoped. He promised solemnly not to come to Newport, or ask us for money again this season; and we were so relieved. For a few days I was almost happy," with a miserable little laugh. "But what fools we were to believe him! I can't imagine why we should, for he has deceived us all through. I don't think he has spoken the truth once from the very beginning. Berry came just now to tell me that he is back already. She saw him herself this morning in Thames Street. He didn't see her, for she was in the close coupé, and he was looking in at a shop window; but, of course, he has come for money, and neither of us has any more. We shall have to refuse, and he will go straight to papa, and then—oh, what will become of me?" She buried her face again in the pillows.

Candace was trembling with a mixture of sensations,— pity for her cousin, indignation at this mean persecution of which she was the victim, and withal a fine touch of scorn over the weakness which was so easily played upon. With all her country breeding and ignorance of the world and its ways, there was in our little maiden a large share of the strong, self-respecting pride of her ancestry. She would never have stooped to buy the silence of a low knave like this Alexander; and her clear truthfulness of soul indicated at once the single, straight, unerring clew which could lead out of this labyrinth of difficulties.

"Georgie," she said, after a moment's thought, "there is just one thing for you to do. You must tell Cousin Kate all about this."

"Oh, Candace, never!" screamed Georgie. "Tell mamma! Have mamma know! I'd rather die at once. You have no idea how she despises concealments and deceits; and I have had to plot and contrive, almost to tell lies, all through this wretched time. She would never get over it. Even if she said she forgave me, I should always read a sort of contempt in her eyes whenever she looked at me. Oh, mamma, mamma! And I love her so! Candace, I couldn't."

"It is the only way," repeated Candace, firmly.

"You have promised not to tell!" exclaimed her cousin, starting up from her recumbent position. "You promised me solemnly! You'll not forget that, will you, Cannie? You'll not tell mother yourself?"

"Certainly not. What use would it be for me to tell her? It would be only next best to having Alexander do it. But you,—you, Georgie,—that is a different thing."

"Even Gertrude said she couldn't advise me to tell mamma," continued Georgie.

"Gertrude! Does Gertrude know about it then?"

"Yes; I had to tell somebody, I was so miserable. It was only a little while ago that I told her. I kept it to myself for a long time."

"Gertrude!" repeated Candace, unable to hide her amazement. "And what did she say?"

"Oh, she was horrified, of course. Any one would be; and she threw a great deal of blame on Berry. I don't think she has ever liked her since. She always goes out of the room when she comes. She wanted me to do all sorts of impossible things, such as going to the chief of police. But about mamma, she felt just as I did. You see we both think so much of mamma, Cannie; we care so much about having her approve of us. You haven't any mother; so perhaps you can't understand."

"No," said Candace, "I have no mother. Perhaps it makes a difference. But there is another thing I can't understand, and that is how girls who have a mother—such a mother as yours, Georgie—can be content to keep her love by means of a cheat. If I did have a mother, I should want her to know all about me, and approve of me honestly, not because I was hiding things from her. Besides,"—there was a little choke here,—"I think mothers can stand a good deal, and still keep on loving their children. I don't believe Cousin Kate would be hard on you, Georgie, or despise you because you have been foolish."

"You don't half know mamma," repeated Georgie. "She has such high ideas about conduct. It would half kill her to know that I had even spoken to a man like this Alexander."

"Of course she would be sorry," persisted Candace. "Of course she would rather that you had never got into this scrape. But she is so just always, as well as kind. She always sees both sides. She will understand how it began,—that Berry over-persuaded you—"

"What makes you say that?" interrupted Georgie. "I never told you that Berry over-persuaded me."

"No; but I knew it all the same. It's a matter of course," said Candace, too deeply in earnest to pick her words, or realize what a very uncomplimentary thing she was saying, "Berry Joy always makes you do whatever she likes. Cousin Kate will realize how it was in a minute."

"Well, never mind that. I want to talk about mamma. Don't you see that if I did tell her she couldn't do anything unless she told papa? and that is the very thing I want to prevent. Oh, what was that?" as the clock began to strike. "Six! They will be here in ten minutes. Oh, dear! how can I meet her? My eyes are swelled out of my head. She will be sure to notice." And Georgie hurried to the looking-glass, and began to smooth the tangled fluffs of hair on her forehead.

Cannie's heart was hot within her, but she wisely forbore further remonstrance. She brought a basin of water and a sponge, and helped Georgie to bathe and cool her tear-stained face, and to arrange her dishevelled locks. Then she kissed her softly, and moved across the room to the window.

Georgie stole after her, and stood by her side. It was nearly time for the travellers to arrive from the train. A cool sea-wind was stirring. Through the trees a red glow could be seen in the west, where the sun was nearing the horizon.

There was a sound of wheels, and the Frewens' village-cart drove rapidly in and set Marian down on the porch. As it drove away, another carriage met and passed it at the gate. It was the coupé, and Mrs. Gray and Gertrude were inside. With a shriek of joy Marian shot down the gravel walk to meet them. John stopped his horses, Mrs. Gray jumped out, and Marian sprang into her arms. The lookers-on at the window above could see the whole pretty picture,—the lovely sunny-faced mother, the glad child; they could hear Mrs. Gray's sweet laugh as she bent over and kissed Marian again and again.

"Oh, Georgie, Georgie," cried Candace, her eyes suddenly brimming over with tears, "look at that, look at them! Was there ever any one so sweet and loving and dear as Cousin Kate? See how she holds Marian in her arms, how she kisses her! How can you be afraid of her? How can you doubt one minute that she loves you enough to forgive anything? Oh, if I had such a mother, would I stay away from her, and cheat and conceal, and trust a girl like Berry Joy, and a bad man like this Alexander, and not trust her?—not go to her first of all for help and advice? Think how good and kind she is, how glad to help everybody,—poor people, servants;

think how lovely she has been to me,—and, of course, she loves you a hundred times more! How can you hesitate one minute? Oh, go straight to her, dear, dear Georgie; tell her all about it, your own self. She will know just what to do. She will make it all right for you. Think how happy you will be not to be afraid of anything any more. Oh, Georgie, do, do!"

"Why, Candace, I hardly know you," faltered Georgie; and she spoke truly, for Candace in her intense eagerness seemed to grow out of and beyond herself, and looked taller, older, quite unlike the shy Candace of every day. Then the passion of her appeal caught hold of Georgie's weakness. Deep feeling is contagious, and there are moments when cowards become temporarily brave. Candace's rush of words, her mother's tender look and attitude as she held Marian close to her, or, it may be, some swift impulse from her good angel, seemed to melt her out of her mood of resistance. How it happened she could not have told, she never could tell; but a sudden strength came to her, and the next moment she was out in the hall. Mrs. Gray, slowly coming upstairs, was clasped in a wild, despairing embrace.

"Oh, mamma! I want you. Oh, mamma! I've something to tell you," cried Georgie. Her mother, whose smile had changed to a look of pale amazement, could not speak. She suffered herself to be swept away. The door of Georgie's room closed behind them; and Gertrude, who was following close behind, was left on the landing to confront the equally surprised Candace.

"What is it? What is Georgie going to say to mamma?" demanded Gertrude, in a frightened whisper.

"She is going to tell her about that horrible man who has been making her so unhappy," replied Candace.

"Going to tell mamma! oh, how did she ever get courage?"

"I begged her—I told her it was the only way."

"You! why, Cannie, how did you dare?" cried Gertrude. "I never would have ventured to do that."

"So Georgie said," replied Candace, simply; "but I was sure the thing to do was for her to go straight to Cousin Kate."

CHAPTER XI.
FIVE AND ONE MAKE SIX.

A long hush followed these few words of explanation. Gertrude was too stunned to ask further questions. Mechanically she moved toward her room, and took off her hat and coat; but all the time she was washing her hands and smoothing her hair, her ears were strained for sounds from Georgie's room, which was next her own. There was very little to be heard,—only a low, continuous murmur of conversation, broken now and then by a louder word; but all so subdued that Candace, sitting on the staircase seat, caught nothing. Marian, rushing up after her mother, had been stopped by the explanation that Georgie was not well, and wanted to be alone with mamma. After a little natural outburst of impatience, she too seemed to catch the vague sense of crisis that was in the air, and settled down quietly, with her head on Candace's knee, to wait.

It was a long waiting. The red sunset sky faded into pallor, and the stars came out. Gertrude, restless with suspense, joined the other two. Both she and Candace were too nervous for ordinary talk, and Marian's presence precluded any mention of the subject with which their thoughts were full; so the trio sat mostly in silence. Frederic was heard to pass down the upper entry and announce dinner; but Mrs. Gray only answered by the word "Presently," and did not open the door. The shadows grew darker as the dusk deepened, till after a while the gas in the hall was lighted, when they fled to the remoter corners, and consoled themselves by casting an added blackness wherever they were permitted to fall,—the only consolation possible to shadows.

To the anxious watchers on the window bench the time seemed very long; and in fact it was nearly eight o'clock before Georgie's door was heard to open, and Mrs. Gray to pass across the hall to her own room. She only stayed there a few minutes. The girls sprang up to receive her as she came downstairs, and the older ones looked anxiously in her face. She was tired and paler than usual, and her eyes showed that she had been crying; but her smile was brave and clear as she put her arm round Candace, and gave her a long kiss.

"You must be half starved, my dears," she said. "Georgie has a bad headache, and I have sent her to bed. She won't come down again to-night; we will have dinner at once."

They went to dinner, accordingly. Marian held fast to her mother's hand; but Mrs. Gray kept the other arm round Candace, and there was a warmth and tenderness in the touch which thrilled through Cannie's heart. She felt, without asking why, that Cousin Kate loved her more than usual that night, and it made her happy.

Jane had been deeply aggrieved at the long delay of the dinner; but she was a woman of resources as well as principle, and, as a member in good and regular standing of the Second Baptist Church, knew that forgiveness of injuries was a branch of Christian duty. She reminded herself, beside, that "Missis wasn't often that inconsiderate, and most probably there was reasons this time," which made it easier to overlook her offence. So she kept some things back, and took some things off, and managed to send in the food in an eatable condition, instead of letting it calcine into cinders as a less conscientious and capable cook would have done.

Marian went to bed; but still Mrs. Gray said not a word about Georgie and her confession. She looked weary and preoccupied, and Gertrude fancied—but perhaps it was only fancy—that there was a shade of coldness in her mother's manner towards herself. They were all glad when the time came to separate; but before she slept that night, Mrs. Gray sent a telegram to her husband.

Mr. Gray appeared next day on the earliest possible train. There was a long consultation in the library, in which Georgie took a part. She came out with her eyes red with crying, but somehow looking relieved, too, and with a peaceful look in her face which had been absent from it of late. Candace, passing her on the stairs, averted her eyes shyly, and was altogether astonished at being caught in a tight embrace and kissed several times.

"It's all right," Georgie whispered. "Papa has been, oh, so kind! and mamma is like an angel to me. You were just right; and I never can thank you enough, you dear!"

"Oh, how glad I am!" cried Cannie, clasping her hands together in sudden relief.

Georgie said no more; she gave Cannie another kiss, and hurried away.

What steps Mr. Gray took to get rid of Alexander, the girls never knew; but whatever they may have been, they were effectual. He disappeared from Newport the very next day, and neither Berry Joy nor Georgie ever saw or heard of him again. It is only on women and girls, and men who are as weak and uninstructed as women, that rascals of his low stamp venture to practise their arts. The moment a man of boldness and resource appears on the scene, one who knows the laws and is not afraid to invoke their protection, black-mailers quail and vanish.

Such an affair cannot, however, be made straight without a good deal of suffering to all concerned. Georgie was forgiven. She was saved from the consequences of her own folly and imprudence; but she could not forgive herself, nor could she forget the deep pain and mortification she had given to the parents she loved, or ignore the fact that she had forfeited something of their good opinion, and that it would take her a long time to regain it. Gertrude, too, had her share to endure. She had a strong sense of honor and a high opinion of her own powers; yet in this the first real test of her life, she had failed miserably, and not only given Georgie no assistance, but had helped to confirm her in her error. Berenice Joy received her portion of punishment in the shape of an interview, which she found most disagreeable, with Mr. Gray. At her urgent entreaty, he gave up his intention of telling the story to her mother, but she felt that she was disgraced in his eyes and in those of Mrs. Gray; and though she cried, and looked very pretty, and was properly grateful and distressed, and assured Mr. Gray that she should never forget how good he had been to her, and that he couldn't imagine how much she and Georgie had suffered just for a moment of thoughtlessness, she was aware all the time that her tears and her gratitude made no impression, and that he did not believe in her. She was sure that all intimacy between herself and Georgie would be discouraged thenceforward; and this was a real punishment, for Berry counted a good deal on the Grays, and had built some social hopes on her position as their friend. Her forebodings proved true. Her little gush of thankfulness and penitence did not touch Mr. Gray's heart in the least. He saw that Berry was a dangerous friend for his soft-hearted, easily influenced Georgie, and told his wife that he decidedly objected to the girls' having anything more to do with her. Mrs. Gray agreed with him in opinion; and though there was no open rupture between the families, Berry found herself after that placed on the footing of an ordinary acquaintance, and was never able to regain her old position with any of the Gray family.

But before this conversation took place it was finally settled that Candace was to stay always, and be Cousin Kate's fourth daughter, and a sister to her three cousins.

Parents, sisters, home,—this was a rich endowment, indeed, for a lonely, orphaned girl to fall heir to. But Cannie had earned her good fortune, and every member of the family had learned to value and to wish to keep her.

It was Mrs. Gray who broke the happy news to her.

"Shall you like it? Will you be content to stay with us always?" she asked.

"Why, Cousin Kate, what a question! How could I help liking it? I never knew what happy meant, till I came to you," answered Cannie, flushed with emotion and pleasure. "It's only that it seems too good to be true! Why, only yesterday I was counting the days till the fifteenth of October; because, you know, you are going back to town then, and I thought you would send me back to Aunt Myra, and I said, 'I shall only be happy for twenty-four days more, perhaps only twenty-three,'—for, you see, I didn't feel sure that you could keep me till the very last day. And now there is going to be no end to the happy times. I can't see what makes you so good to me, Cousin Kate."

"I think we can understand that better than you can," her cousin replied. "We need you, Cannie, as much as you need us. The benefit will be mutual."

"Need me! when you have Cousin Court and the girls?"

"Cousin Court and the girls need you too.—Don't we, Georgie? Come in and help me explain to Candace that all of us want her, and all of us are glad to have her stay."

"Indeed, we do. Cannie, I can't talk about it, for it's like a bad dream from which I have waked up, and I don't like to recall it; but I never shall forget how good you were to me that horrible day. It was you who persuaded me to go to mamma. I never should have gone if you hadn't somehow swept me up and made me. And, oh, if I hadn't!—How could I be afraid of you, dear, darling mamma?—She was just what you said she would be, Cannie. She knew just what to do; she understood in a moment. She was so kind! I feel as if Trinity Church had been rolled off my mind. It was all your doing, and I never can forget it."

"Georgie is right," said Mrs. Gray. "Don't look so bewildered, dear. You did her a real service in persuading her to be brave and frank. I don't know why it is so hard for children to trust their parents. It is the parents' fault somehow, no doubt."

"Oh, mother, no! It was only that I dreaded to have you think ill of me."

"Not quite," said Mrs. Gray, shaking her head. "I must blame myself a little. I must have made some mistake with you all, when even Gertrude could not believe that I would not be harsh and unforgiving. But we have had our lesson, Georgie, and we will not do so badly again, especially as there will be this dear little new sister of yours to help us to keep straight. We need not talk any more about it, but, Cannie, we all feel that to have you with us will be good for us all. There is nothing in the world so rare and so precious as clear truth, and the courage to hold fast by it; and we have proved that you possess both."

"And don't you think that it will be good for me?" said Cannie, her eyes shining with grateful tears.

"Yes; we can help you too. It is one of the good things in this world that help is almost always on both sides.— Marian," as that small person passed the door, "what do you think of having Cannie permanently for a sister?"

"Really! Will she stay? Oh, how perfectly—daisy!" And Marian threw her arms round Candace's neck, and gave her a squeeze which left no doubt as to her approval of the plan.

Only one cloud now remained on Candace's horizon of happiness. Mrs. Gray had become like a very mother to her. Her bright, perpetual, all-understanding tenderness was like daily food to Candace's hungering heart. Mr. Gray had taken her into the highest favor. He had always liked Cannie and been kind to her, but now he petted her almost as much as he petted Marian. He scarcely ever came back from New York without bringing her some little gift,—a book, a trinket, a box of bonbons,—as a proof that she had been in his thoughts. The latest and prettiest of these was on her finger now,—a pearl ring with the word "Truth" engraved inside its golden circlet. Georgie and Marian had welcomed her heartily; but Gertrude,—Gertrude had said nothing. She was always cordial now, and a sort of added respect and liking had appeared in her manner since the Alexander episode; but about the new arrangement which made Candace one of the family, she had not spoken a word. Till she did, till she was sure that Gertrude too was content to have her stay, Cannie's happiness could not be complete.

The fourteenth of October at length arrived. It was the last day of their Newport season, but Candace no longer dreaded the break-up. It did not mean separation and loneliness now, only the change to a new and different scene, which might be as delightful in its way as the summer had been. Yet Newport was still in full beauty, and it seemed a pity to leave it. No frosts had fallen to dim the glory of the flowers. The honeysuckles were still starred with their white, gold-anthered blossoms; the geranium beds looked as gay, the foliage plants as superb as ever; while the green of the grass was as fresh as in July. Here and there a little drift of yellow leaves lay under the trees, but it was the only sign of autumn. Georgie gathered a great basketful of nasturtiums, heliotrope, and mignonette to carry down to Miss Gisborne, and Marian was sent off in the village-cart with a similar basketful for Mrs. Frewen. The house was all in a confusion of packing. Frederic was wrapping tissue-paper round the picture-frames, Elizabeth counting linen and silver, the gardeners emptying the balcony boxes. Mrs. Gray proposed that Gertrude and Candace should go for a last walk on the Cliffs, and so be out of the way of these discomforts.

"There is nothing for you to do," she said. "Only don't stay too late, and come in before it grows dark. We are to have a 'thick tea' at half-past six, in place of a regular dinner. I thought it would be less trouble on this busy day."

It was to Pulpit Rock that the two cousins bent their way. The Cliffs were even lonelier now than they had been when Candace first visited them. There were no bathers in the surf; no carriages were drawn up on the higher part of the beach, and the road leading around Easton's Point showed only a few scattered figures and one solitary horseman on its entire length. Here and there along the windings of the Cliff Walk a single walker appeared, dark against the brightness of the sky, or two girls were seen pacing the smooth gravel, with fluttering dresses, and hair blown by the soft October wind. The sea was as beautiful in color as ever, but it had changed with the change of the season. The blue seemed more rarefied, the opalescent tints more intense; deep purple reflections lay in the shadows made by the rocky points, and there was a bright clearness of atmosphere quite unlike the dream-like mistiness of the summer.

The cousins sat side by side on the big rock, just where they had sat on that June day which seemed to Candace so long ago. Gertrude was no longer critical or scornful. She sat a little farther back than Candace, and from time to time glanced at her side-face with a sort of puzzled expression. Cannie, happening to turn, caught the look; it embarrassed her a little, and to hide the embarrassment she began to talk.

"Did you know that Cousin Kate is going to let me live with you always?" she asked.

"Yes; mamma told me."

"Isn't she good?" went on Candace, impulsively. "I can hardly believe yet that it is true. What makes you all so very, very kind to me, I can't think."

"I haven't been particularly kind," said Gertrude, suddenly. "Candace,—I might as well say it at once, for it's been a good deal on my mind lately,—I wish you would forget how nasty I was when you first came to us."

"Were you nasty?" said Candace, trying to speak lightly, but with a flush creeping into her face.

"Yes, I was; very nasty. I didn't care to have you come, in the first place; and I thought you seemed awkward and countrified, and I didn't like your clothes, and I was afraid the girls here would laugh at you. It was a mean sort of feeling, and the worst thing is that I didn't see that it was mean. I was ashamed of you; but now I am ashamed, dreadfully ashamed, of myself. I felt so much wiser and more knowing than you then; and yet when Georgie, my own sister, got into this dreadful trouble and came to me for help, I had none to give her. I was as much a coward as she was. I gave her bad advice; and it was you, whom I laughed at and was unkind to, who saw what she ought to do, and was brave and really helped. When I think of it all, I feel as if I couldn't forgive myself."

"Why, Gertrude dear, don't!" cried Cannie; for Gertrude was almost crying. "I don't wonder you didn't care for me at first. I was dreadfully awkward and stupid. And you never were nasty to me. Don't say such things! But"—with a shy longing to remove beyond question the doubt which had troubled her—"you do like me now? You are not sorry that I am to stay and live with you?"

"Sorry! No; I am very, very glad. You are the best girl I know. It will do me heaps of good to have you in the house."

"Oh, how delightful!" cried Cannie. "Now I haven't a thing to wish for. It is all nonsense about my doing you good, but I am so glad you want me to stay."

The two girls nestled closer and kissed each other, with a new sense of friendship and liking. The west wind blew past, making little quick eddies on the surface of the water.

The gulls flew lower, their white wings flashing close to the flashing surf; sails far out at sea gleamed golden in the level rays of the sunset; a yellow light enveloped the farther point.

"I shall always love this rock," said Candace.

Gertrude began the downward climb; but Candace paused a moment on the summit, and turned for a last look at the water. Every glittering foam-cap, every glinting sail, seemed to her to wave a signal of glad sympathy and congratulation. "Good-by," she softly whispered. "But I shall come back. You belong to me now." She kissed her hand to the far blue horizon; then with a smile on her face, she turned, and followed Gertrude down the steep rock-face, a happy girl.

The Cliffs.
"I shall always love this rock," said Candace